THE WELL

NOLEEN SANDERSON

The Well

Endorsements for

THE WELL

I absolutely love this story.

We don't know a lot about the Samaritan woman at the well and reading this book kept me so captivated and longing to find out what was going to happen next. I also absolutely loved the Scripture and the poetry that is woven through this book. It's just so beautiful & makes the story even more special to read.

A book I could not put down & will definitely read again.

Donna Spence
Co-Founder of VANA Ministries

Noleen has the ability to make a story set in the time of biblical Samaria or modern day central Palestine come to life in the modern age by narrating the story of the woman at the well in an everyday and relatable way. It is the story of a young girl that reveals the best and the worst of relationships and of circumstances that can happen to any one of us, regardless of time and place. She reveals with heartbreaking honesty how relationships and religion can damage and break a person though hurt, pain, grief, abuse, despair and shame. But it is also a story of survival, of thirst for something better, of hope and courage and of real love and forgiveness, all told in a captivating manner.

Highly recommended.

Vivienne Riches
Clinical professor, psychologist,
BA, Dip.Ed., MA(hons), PhD, FASID

This book is dedicated to
the woman Jesus met at Jacob's well.
Broken and hurting, yet authentic and real.
Her life is a legacy that still echos today.
May those who read this story,
find their hope etched in deep and living waters,
just as she did.

Contents

Samaritans *are an ethnoreligious group descending from the northern Israelite tribes of Ephraim and Manasseh. The northern kingdom of Israel, with its capital Samaria, and the southern Kingdom of Judah, with Jerusalem as its capital, were united under King Solomon, and at that time, it was almost impossible (even for rabbis) to draw a clear distinction between Samaritanism and Judaism.*

However, after Solomon's death, a rift developed between the two groups. Although the exact circumstances surrounding the schism are unclear, the Assyrian conquest over the Kingdom of Israel in 722 B.C. appears to have played a major role.

Large numbers of southern Israelites were taken to Assyria as slaves. The Assyrians also introduced other ethnic groups into northern Israel. As a result of this potential mingling of the Israeli bloodlines with foreigners on both sides, mistrust between Jews and Samaritans intensified as each group considered theirs to be the pure Israeli bloodline and viewed the other as a race of half-casts.

By the time of Christ, the feud had grown to such intensity that the Jews regularly crossed the Jordan river to avoid contact with Samaritans – choosing to follow a longer and more arduous route, rather than travelling through Samaria.

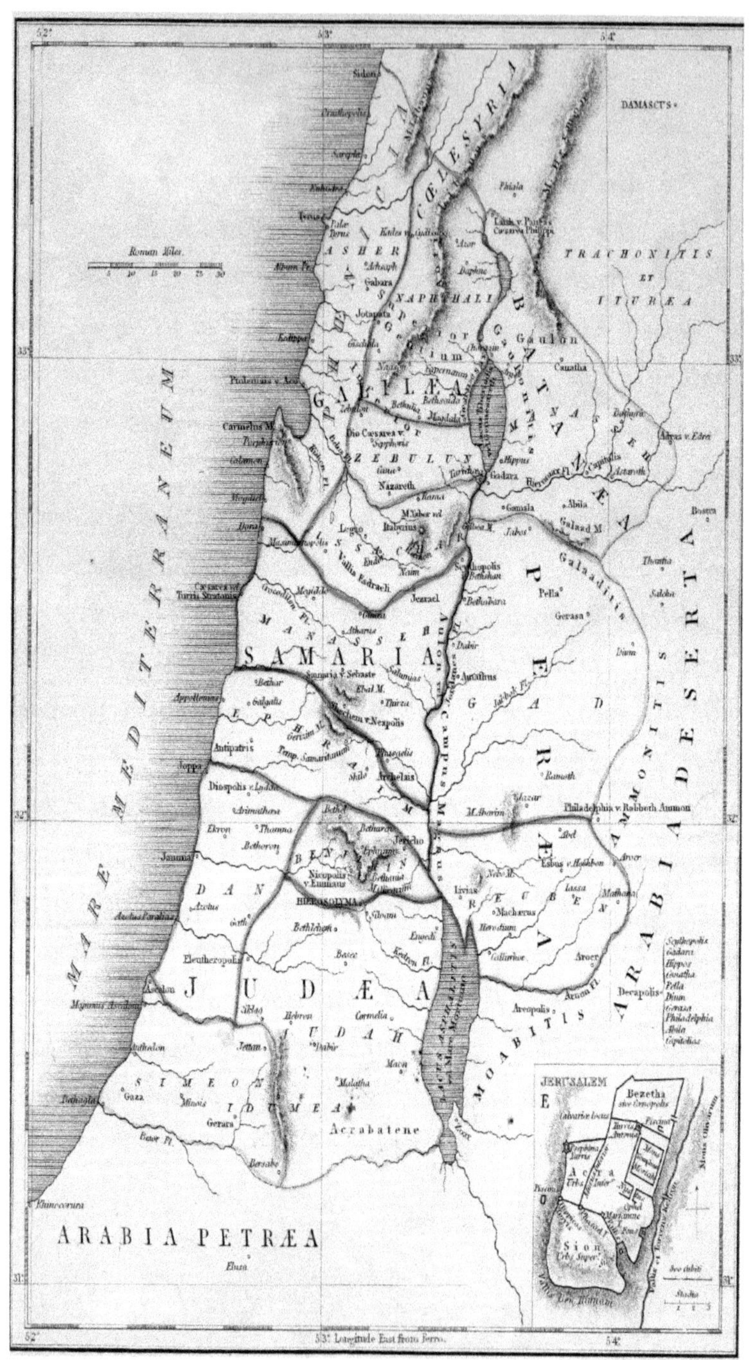

DAMASCVS
TRACHONITIS ET ITVRÆA
CŒLESYRIA
Sidon
Sarepta
Tyrus
Phiala
Laus v. Pan
Cæsarea Philippi
Palæ Tyrus
ASHER
Ahzaph
Gabara
NAPHTHALI
Jotapata
GAULON
Canatha
Ptolemais v. Acco
GALILÆA
Capernaum
BATANÆA
Carmelus M.
Dio Cæsarea v. Sepphoris
ZEBULUN
Tarichea
Hippus
Gadara
Hieromax Fl.
Scythopolis
Nazareth
Gamala
Abila
Gilead M.
Galaad M.
Bostra
M. Tabor vel Itabyrius
Endor
Naim
Scythopolis
Bethshan
Pella
Gerasa
Dium
MANASSES
SAMARIA
Samaria v. Sebaste
Ebal M.
Thirza
Bethabara
Antipatris
Sichem v. Neapolis
GAD
Jabbok Fl.
Joppa
Shilo
Archelais
Diospolis v. Lydda
Arimathæa
M. Abarim
Philadelphia v. Rabboth Ammon
Ekron
Thamna
Jericho
Bethoron
BENJAMIN
Nicopolis v. Emmaus
HIEROSOLYMA
Silvan
Nebo M.
Esbus v. Hesbon
Azotus
Gath
Bethlehem
REUBEN
Machærus
Ascalon
JUDÆA
JUDAH
Hebron
Carmelia
SIMEON
Gaza
IDUMÆA
Gerara
Acrabatene
MARE MEDITERRANEUM
ARABIA DESERTA
AMMONITIS
MOABITIS
ARABIA PETRÆA
Rhinocorura
Elusa
Roman Miles
Longitude East from Ferro

JERUSALEM
Bezetha sive Cœnopolis
Acra
Sion

Prelude

There is something truly beautiful
About imperfect people.
The rough-around-the-edges
And the not-quite-good-enoughs.

They are the so-called misfits
Who feel perpetually alone,
For they became lost in the wilderness
And never found their way home.

They are the wallflowers who linger
At the edges of a crowd.
The ones who never even try
To make their voices loud.

There is something truly beautiful
About the cracked and broken.
About those who know their flaws,
But don't hide them away.

For life is not a showroom,
And most people not designed
To live like stuffed mannequins
On perpetual display.

We are wild.
We are messy.
We are infinitely complicated.
We are shattered in places
No light of day will ever see.

We carry wounds like rivers
That run through underground canyons,
With a pressure so strong
It could defy gravity.

Down deep in the canyons,
Way beneath the surface,
Is the source of your own
Pure artesian spring.

But you will never taste the flow
If life is too crowded,
By endless demands of perfectionism
From trying to fit in.

The pressure on all sides
propels you forward,
Through the jagged impatient teeth
Of the earth's rocks below.

It is a call deep within,
A drumming whispered heartbeat,
That begs you to be
As wildly free as the wind.

BE your perfectly-imperfect.
BE your beautifully broken.
Let your rusty voice sing
Like a bird in the trees.

Live your life without apology,
And with wild abandon,
For you weren't created for a cage,
You were made to fly free.

You are one of a kind.
The rarest of jewels.
And it is through your cracks
That the light filters in.

So, breathe and now know
That harmony is found,
In the pieces of your soul
That weren't made to fit in.

Miriam – age 43

Miriam sat on the edge of the stone wall that encircled the well. A hot breeze blew swirls of dust particles around her sandaled feet.

What day was it? She couldn't recall, even though she tried counting forward from the last Sabbath. Had it been three or four days since then? The days, as usual, had all blurred together.

Miriam was exhausted. With a sigh, she acknowledged her fatigue like one might nod to an old acquaintance. She knew it wasn't because of the walk from town to the well. A walk made more arduous now that she had been forced to do it in the heat of the midday sun. The walk was simply part of her daily routine. From some of her earliest memories, days began with a walk to the well to fetch water for the household.

No, today's exhaustion was not the result of her physical labour, or the fact that she had been awake since before the sunrise, despite tossing and turning all night. She blinked against the grittiness that dust and sleep deprivation left in her eyes. She was used to hard work, and sadly, she was also used to not sleeping properly.

The true cause of her exhaustion was just as old and just as familiar. Its name was *shame*. It coiled around her as tightly as a python might, leaving her feeling powerless and incapacitated. It sucked the energy right out of her bones. These days, she felt that she had no strength left for the fight.

Dropping the pitcher gently into the well, she watched as it descended into the cool enticing darkness. There was a gentle splash as it landed at the bottom. She always enjoyed hearing that little splash, as if it were a reassuring message sent from below.

The pitcher would then begin to drown. It didn't take long for the drowning to occur. Just a few moments inside the well, and the water would smother and fill the pitcher completely. She would feel the familiar tension on the rope and know the pitcher was full. Then she would haul on the rope and rescue it.

The drowning and rescuing and drowning again formed a familiar scenario that seemed to echo the story of her life – a story filled with things she wished she could forget.

It would take eight refills of the pitcher before the earthen jar that sat in the dirt at her feet would be full and she could begin the journey home.

Hand over hand she pulled at the rope, the strain reverberated down her back. When the pitcher finally emerged, she grabbed the thin wooden pole suspended over the middle of the well and swung the pitcher towards her outstretched hand.

No sooner had she grasped its slick wet sides, than she became aware of an overwhelming dryness in her throat. She unclipped a scoop from the sash of her tunic and, instead of pouring the water into the earthen jar, she thrust the scoop into the pitcher and brought it brimming with water up to her lips. Miriam closed her eyes as the fresh, clean, clear liquid filled her mouth and gulped it down deeply. It felt so good. She needed more. Another scoop and then another.

"At this rate it will take me nine refills," she muttered under her breath in an effort to convince herself to stop drinking.

Finally, she clipped the scoop back onto her sash and poured the remaining water into the earthen jar. Then she turned back to the well and drowned the pitcher once more.

The sun beat down relentlessly on the roof that sheltered the well from dust and debris. Although Miriam was thankful for the meagre shade it provided, it was entirely ineffective against the heat that rose up from the desert floor.

Miriam sat alone. No one in their right mind would come here in the heat of the day. Not unless there was no other choice.

The village women preferred the cool of the morning; the shepherds, the soft light of evening. For the village women, the outing to the well was as much about gathering the latest gossip as it was about collecting water. It was also their chance to escape the censorious scrutiny of their husbands and extended families. Beside the well, they could unwind and enjoy the fellowship of each other's company. Friendships were woven across time through mutual understanding, and the women fortified one another with strength.

However, some women were excluded from this firmly established social cohesion, and this exclusion could be brutal. Miriam had become one of these women, and as such, she was no longer welcome amongst the women she had once called friends. Though she tried to be philosophical about it, her exile hurt her very deeply.

As she dragged the heavy pitcher back up again, her mind returned to the days when she had been welcomed by the community of women at the well. She had been younger and so full of life back then.

When her mother had finally deemed her old enough to go to the well without her supervision – just as long as she stayed with the other girls – Miriam had relished the task.

Miriam and her friends were sternly warned to stay together and not wander off alone. The desert was an unpredictable place, and young women were vulnerable to attack. 'Living prey,' were the words her father had used. So, in obedience, she had stayed close to her three best friends, Neriah, Sheerah and Mary, on their trips to the well.

A wry smile crossed Miriam's face as she remembered laughing with them over the boys in town. Back then, Sheerah had been in love with a boy called Rueben whom she longed to marry, but her parents had other ideas. Whenever she lamented this situation, her friends would tell jokes until she felt better.

Neriah was the sensible and serious one. She always made sure they didn't linger too long at the well in the evening or get caught after dark on the trail. Even back then, Neriah had been slightly intimidating.

Mary was more like Miriam. Her sense of mischief and cheeky fun often had them in stitches – even Neriah. Mary and Miriam loved to play jokes on people and regale the other girls with stories of their antics. *Oh, the stories!*

Miriam missed her friends, but it was such a long time ago now. She wasn't even the same person – no longer an innocent and naïve young girl, so full of hope for the future, always dreaming of the day when she would be married and living free from her father's constant criticism.

Instead of fulfilling them, the years had shattered her expectations and dreams one by one. Her dreams had become more than disappointments. They had become more than grief and more than pain. They had been held up before her and savagely murdered while she was forced to watch.

In truth, she didn't know *who* she was anymore. Only that her wounds ran jagged, raw and deep, and all too often, she was the one holding the knife.

Her old friends still walked to the well together. Miriam saw them in the early hours of the morning as they passed her shack on the outskirts of town. They spoke in low whispers as they passed by, and though they never looked her way, Miriam felt their disdain burning her skin like hot steam.

She was no longer their friend. Instead, she had become *that woman*. Despised by the other women for being a sinner beyond redemption, simply because she had made a fatal mistake of loving someone she never should have. Now she and her lover were ostracised and her two small children had become pariahs. They were treated worse than stray dogs if they ever ventured into town.

Although she yearned for the companionship they had once shared, Miriam never dared to approach the women. Added to their silent rejection, the shame of their insults would be too much to bear. The defensive walls she'd built around her heart were far too thin and would surely break beneath the strain of their recriminations.

The sound of the pitcher splashing into the water below jolted her back to the present. Was this the fourth or fifth pitcher? She'd lost count. She sighed. *What did it matter?* She was only counting to pass the time and would have to keep going until the earthen jug was full anyway.

She wiped sweat away from her brow, let go of the rope and stood up. Pressing her palms flat against her lower back, she arched her spine to relieve her aching muscles.

As she did so, Miriam scanned her surroundings.

Some distance behind her, the town of Sychar sat nestled amongst the hills that she had come to love as a child. The water well stood like a sentinel outside of the town and its solitude seemed to echo her own. Beyond the well, lay nothing but the endless dry dusty desert with the occasional tree sticking out of the sand like a needle.

Turning her gaze back towards Sychar, she could just distinguish the silhouettes of its buildings through the heat haze that rose like a spectre from the burning sand.

It was much the same as any other Samaritan town, and Miriam still wasn't sure why she had come back here after all these years. Or why she, Michael and the children stayed on, after they had been pushed out of town life and forced to live in a ramshackle building that leaned against the town wall.

Certainly, being away from the painful memories Sychar held for all of them would have been much easier. Perhaps, in a different town, where no one knew her history or could judge her for it, she would be able to escape – at least for a while.

In the past, she had taken that route. Tried to get away from her shame by losing herself in a new place. And there had been brief moments in those faraway towns, when she had been able to stop looking over her shoulder and worrying about whether she might bump into someone she knew. In those brief seasons, she had no longer dreaded the daggered looks of unspoken judgment, the unasked questions, and the fierce accusations that sat on the tongues of everyone in Sychar. She had tasted something that almost felt like freedom.

Why had she come back? And more importantly, why did she stay? The truth was that they just did not have the money – and if she was honest, the energy, to move away. Once her illicit relationship with Michael had come to light, the whole town had turned against them. They had been driven out, stripped of their possessions, including her father's house, and forced to live as outcasts.

Miriam sighed deeply, stretched her arms behind her back and then out to her sides before sitting down again on the edge of the well. Hand over hand she pulled on the rope, wondering how her life had turned out this way. She knew she was to blame, but the more she thought about it, the more the old feelings of resentment and bitterness rose, tangling itself around the shame. They clawed at her soul. *If only … If only … If only …* So many raw regrets filled her chest and as they spilled over, she began to weep.

"No, I don't want to cry again today." She tried to bite back the tears, but as she leaned over to grab the pitcher, she could see them splashing into the fresh water. With both hands occupied hefting the pitcher, she dried her face as best she could on the sleeve of her robe before pouring the water into the earthen jar and tossing the pitcher back down into the hole.

Wiping away the remainder of her tears, Miriam focused on finishing the task. She desperately wanted to be far away from the well and the memories it held of the happy days spent here with her friends. Days she knew she would never have again.

She was so intent on pulling the pitcher to the surface that she didn't notice a group of men walking over the sands towards her. Sandaled, dusty, rough-looking men. If she had seen them, she would have sensed the danger and hurried away without bothering to finish filling the earthen jar.

As their silent steps brought them ever closer across the sand, she sat exposed and vulnerable – a living prey.

Chapter 1

Little Bird

*Samaria was once the central region of the
ancient Kingdom of Israel. It is located
in a beautiful mountainous area with the
Mediterranean Sea to the East and the Jordan
River along its Western flank. To the north lies
Galilee and to the south, Judea.*

Noleen Sanderson

Little bird
Just stand now
High up
In your tree,
And sing with all your heart.
Sing out
Your melody.
For He is in control…
And
You
Cannot fall
Out of His hand.
Your life
Is in His grip,
And He has told you
Just to stand.
Do not fear
The shaking
Of the branches
Down below.
Or the
Howling gale
That rages rough
And billows
As it blows.
No, you just stand
And sing.
Look up
Through the leaves.
For every
Little sparrow's song,
Is sung
When she believes.

Miriam – age 10

While her mother rushed around inside placing bowls beneath leaks in the roof, Miriam sat transfixed with her hands wrapped around her knees under the awning just outside the front door. Rain this heavy was such an unusual and awe-inspiring sight that she was mesmerised by it. Unable to turn her eyes away, she watched it pour down over the desert's sandy hills and bounce off the dry surfaces around the house.

Thunder boomed above, and Miriam involuntarily shivered, hugging her knees tighter to her chest, but she didn't run or stray from her position. Everywhere she glanced was a new wonder that made her gasp in delight.

The rain was so torrential it ran like small rivers off the corners of the roof and into the waiting rain barrels. Some of it splashed up against her legs even though she was perched on an old wooden bench. The water was cool and sent shivers of excitement up and down her spine. She wanted to run and stomp her feet hard into the pools that were rapidly forming around the house. The neighbourhood children were chasing each other around in the downpour and squealing with glee and excitement. Oh, how she longed to join them, but her mother had given her strict instructions not to get her tunic wet.

"You can sit on the chair, but that's all. Do not go out into the rain." Miriam obeyed, but the temptation was overwhelming.

After some time, Miriam's mother surprised her

when she came through the door and sat beside her. "I thought I'd watch the rain with you for a while." Miriam smiled. It was unusual for her mother to stop her chores and spend time with her.

"It's so beautiful Mama. I didn't know it could rain like this."

"Oh, it can rain my girl, believe me. And we need it. It's been years of drought now. With this rain some of our suffering will finally be over. It's an answer to prayer."

"When will it stop?"

Her mother smiled. "When God decides. It is all in His hands. Do you remember me telling you the story of the great flood?"

"Yes, but that's just a story. I've never seen it rain like this before. Like it's flooding."

"Well, it happened once. They called it the great flood. The ancient scripts tell us that people lived much longer before the flood than they do now. My father told me that before the great flood there was water above the sky. God Almighty warned Noah that the flood was coming and told him to build an ark. Thankfully for all of us alive today, Noah obeyed and saved his family. Everyone else was drowned in the waters that swallowed up the whole earth."

"Why would God destroy everyone, Mama? Does he hate people so much?"

Her mother stared at the rivers pouring from the corners of the roof. "No, my dear, I don't think so. I think he hated what the people did. They had turned their backs on him and no longer listened to him. They thought they could live any way they wanted. They did lots of terrible things, and they didn't care about God anymore."

"What sorts of things?"

"Well, they worshiped false gods and ignored God's commandments. God is holy and cannot tolerate sin, so I guess he finally had enough. But he saved Noah, which means he didn't hate people because he chose to save those who would listen and obey."

"Oh." Miriam didn't know if she really believed the story, but she liked listening to the sound of her mother's voice. "What if the rain doesn't stop Mama? Will God send another flood? Is he angry with people again?" She couldn't help but imagine her house going underwater and her family downing.

Her mother tussled the dark curls that fell down Miriam's back. "No, my girl. God promised Noah that he would never do that again. He sent a rainbow as a reminder of his promise. Perhaps we will see one after the rain stops."

Miriam nodded. She liked seeing her mother relaxed and happy. They sat in companionable silence watching the rain until it finally relented and the dark clouds moved away. But that afternoon the rainbow never came. Something else arrived instead. Something, or rather someone, Miriam had learnt to dread.

Miriam's father stomped into the house. He was in a foul mood. As was common, his loud voice and unpredictable behaviour terrified Miriam. The words he spat at his wife and child were as painful as any fist might have been. In her short ten years of life, Miriam's heart had been significantly bruised and shattered by her father's anger.

That rain-soaked afternoon was no different. The tyrant marched into their home, unleashing an overwhelming fury that filled every crack and corner.

"Go outside and play," whispered her mother.

"But—"

"I said, 'Go.' Now, get out."

Miriam fled. Past her friends' homes, past the market, past the town gates, through the pastures and up into the foothills. The familiar path, usually dry and edged with brittle yellow grass, was slippery from the rain. Mud lapped at the hem of her tunic. Still, she ran on. She ran until her father's voice no longer echoed in her ears.

She knew she shouldn't be up here, but she did not want the company of her friends. How could she tell them about her father's blind rage, and her weakness and inability to protect her mother?

She reached the top of the hill and scrambled onto the large flat rock that was her favourite thinking spot.

She loved sitting up here, looking down on the houses. It made her feel closer to the God her mother spoke about. Now, she curled her knees up to her chest and crossed her arms over them. She rested her head on her folded arms and prayed fervently to God that her father would just go away. She thought perhaps she hated him. She was sure *he* hated her. She had seen it in his eyes.

As she sat and rocked, she thought of all the horrible names he had ever called her. *Stupid. Dumb. Useless. Lazy. No-good. Annoying. Always in the way.* They came back to haunt her at times like this. Like lions crouching just beyond the campfire's reach, they waited on the edge of her consciousness until another brush with his rage gave them reason to attack her once more.

She couldn't think of one nice thing he'd ever said to her. He had certainly never told her he loved her, but she didn't understand why he hated her so much.

The tears came then. The more she thought about his unkind words, the more she cried. It felt good to let it all out.

After a time, her crying simmered down to a whimper. She slid her hands across the surface of the rock. Its unchanging features were as reassuring and familiar to her as the lines of her mother's face. She had no adequate words to express the comfort the rock gave her. Time seemed to slow down, the pain gradually subsided, and she fell into a peaceful trance, tracing the grooves and edges of the rock with her finger.

Suddenly, a voice from behind jerked her out of her reverie.

"Hello Miriam. Are you alright?" Miriam jumped up and turned to face the speaker.

"Sorry, I didn't mean to startle you."

"Oh, hello Michael." She rubbed her face to rid it of any residual tears. Rock dust left grimy smudges on her cheeks. The shepherd boy stood awkwardly at the edge of the rock, a frown on his young face.

"What's wrong? Have you been crying?"

"No. Nothing's wrong."

"I heard someone crying a while back from way over there," he pointed to the pasture at the base of the hill. "So, I came to see ..."

"Well, it wasn't me." She was defensive.

Miriam envied Michael. He could roam free in these hills every day and tend to his little flock of sheep with no one telling him what to do. The first time Miriam met him, she had been gathering wildflowers and had stopped to sit on her rock for a while when he came up the hill followed by a dozen sheep. She could barely hear his greeting over their bleating.

People in town looked down on the shepherds because they were a rough bunch who smelled of the animals they tended, but Miriam had become fond of Michael despite his sheep-smell. An easy friendship had grown between them.

Michael was different from the boys in town who either teased her or ignored her completely. He was kind and took the time to talk to her even though she was just a girl.

Now he looked at her curiously. "You sure about that? I could have sworn I heard someone crying."

Not trusting herself to speak, she nodded.

"I see. Well, as long as you're okay…"

"I'm fine." She tried a reassuring smile. It wobbled a little, but it held.

"Hey, do you know what happened to us today?" He waved his hand in the direction of his flock. "The lot of us got caught in that rainstorm. We're all soaked to the skin." She looked him up and down then and realised his brown tunic was sodden. Water still dripped from the tassels of its sash. His unruly curls hung in wet clumps around his face. Aware of her gaze, he tried to push a fallen lock into place behind his ear, but it had a mind of its own and sprang back in rebellion. That made her smile.

"Oh, you think that's funny?" he teased, shaking his head back and forth like a shaggy dog after a swim.

Droplets landed on her arms. "Stop that." She giggled and brushed them away.

"Just look at my poor bedraggled sheep. They are ever-so grumpy. They blame me, you see, but I hardly had time to get us all to shelter as that rain came in so fast. This lot were scared witless. They ran right over me. It was all I could do to keep up with them." Miriam looked over at the sheep. Their thick coats were drenched and their big eyes stared forlornly out of wet woollen faces.

As though they were in on the conversation, the sheep started a fresh round of mournful bleating. Miriam laughed. "It certainly sounds like they blame you for the rain."

"Oo," Michael pretended to be afraid of the sheep as he looked over at them. "They look so mad. Save me, Miriam." He made his knees knock together comically and tried to hide behind his staff, peeping around at the sheep from time to time, and then squealing when he saw them.

"Oh Michael, I'm sorry, but I don't think anything can protect you from those upset sheep."

Thunder rumbled ominously in the distance. Michael straightened. The smile left his face as he peered at the sky. "Hmm. Those dark clouds on the horizon are coming this way. Looks like we're in for another good drenching tonight. Let's get going. I'm taking my sheep down to their pen before they revolt." He jerked his head in the sheep's direction without looking at her and rolled his eyes. Miriam couldn't help but giggle.

"How about we walk down together?"

Miriam nodded reluctantly. She didn't want to go home, but she did not want to get caught in the storm either. She hoped her father would not still be in a rage. Her steps were deliberately slow as she followed Michael down the steep bank. He noticed her lagging.

"Come on little sis," he urged, and when she showed no sign of hurrying up, he headed over and crouched down with his back to her. "Here, jump on my back and I'll carry you down."

Miriam put her arms around his neck, and Michael piggybacked her down the hillside. She felt the strength of his shoulders and liked the sensation of being cared for by a friend. She felt safe and protected. Why couldn't her father be more like this shepherd boy?

At a fork in the trail, he put her down.

"There you are. Now go on little sis. Hurry up and get home before that rain comes again." Michael smiled as he used his staff to push Miriam gently in the direction of her home like he might manoeuvre one of his sheep. Then he and his flock of rain-soaked sheep took a different path. She stood for a moment and watched him go.

Chapter II

Nothing More Powerful

Jacob's well is a deep well carved into bedrock.
It is situated near the ancient town of Sychar in Samaria.
The well has been associated in religious tradition with
Jacob for approximately two millennia. It is the place where
Jacob, one of the founding fathers of the faith, is said to
have met his wife Rachel.

Genesis 29: 1-12 (NASB)

Then Jacob set out on his journey and went to the land of the people of the east. He looked, and saw a well in the field, and behold, three flocks of sheep were lying there beside it, because they watered the flocks from that well. Now the stone on the mouth of the well was large. When all the flocks were gathered there, they would roll the stone from the mouth of the well and water the sheep. Then they would put the stone back in its place on the mouth of the well.

Jacob said to them, "My brothers, where are you from?" And they said, "We are from Haran." So, he said to them, "Do you know Laban the son of Nahor?" And they said, "We know him." And he said to them, "Is it well with him?" And they said, "It is well, and here is his daughter Rachel coming with the sheep." Then he said, "Look, it is still high day; it is not time for the livestock to be gathered. Water the sheep, and go, pasture them." But they said, "We cannot, until all the flocks are gathered, and they roll the stone from the mouth of the well; then we water the sheep."

While he was still speaking with them, Rachel came with her father's sheep, for she was a shepherdess. When Jacob saw Rachel the daughter of his mother's brother Laban, and the sheep of his mother's brother Laban, Jacob went up and rolled the stone from the mouth of the well and watered the flock of his mother's brother Laban. Then Jacob kissed Rachel and raised his voice and wept. Jacob told Rachel that he was a relative of her father and that he was Rebekah's son, and she ran and told her father.

There is nothing more powerful than a little kindness.
There is nothing that can outrun grace.
There is nothing as reassuring as friendship.
There is nothing that is stronger than faith.
One will determine the course that you set.
One will hoist up the sails.
One will navigate by the stars above.
One will simply refuse to fail.

Together they are a force to be
reckoned with.
Together they will not be knocked down.
Together they with sail straight
into the storm.
Together they will get you to solid ground.

You'll see them even in the little things.
You'll see them in every day.
You'll see them when you least expect it.
You'll see them as you journey your way.

Kindness is like water to the thirsty.
Grace is the power to heal.
Friendship is unconditional acceptance.
Faith makes the vision real.

Don't ever take them for granted.
Don't think you can go it alone.
Hold them close to your heart
And allow them to lead you home.

Miriam – age 13

Jacob's well was large and deep. For countless decades, it yielded an abundant supply of life-giving water to the surrounding tribes, towns, and weary travellers. Whether there was rain or drought, the well never ran dry or diminished. Without it, Sychar could not exist.

In the cool evenings, shepherds from the surrounding regions came to the well to water their flocks, but at sunrise, it was the domain of the women of Sychar. Miriam cherished the mornings that her mother would wake her up before sunrise to join them on their journey out to the well. There was something exciting about getting up while the rest of the world was still sleeping and walking straight out into the changing light. Oranges and pinks glowed softly in the foothills and danced across the sand, taking her breath away.

Her mother carried the empty earthen jar on top of her head – a skill Miriam was yet to master, though her mother, her back straight and strong and her head held high, made it look effortless. To Miriam, she was the picture of dignity and beauty.

When Miriam was thirteen, her mother had finally granted her permission to walk to the well unaccompanied. She had been one of the last in her group of friends to achieve this longed-for status. She could not wait to take on her new role.

"As you are a woman now Miriam, it is time for you to take more responsibility. This could be one of the last times I will accompany you to the well. From tomorrow, you will join the other women and carry the jar yourself."

"Yes, Mama." Miriam agreed in her most grown-up voice, trying her best not to squeal with glee. At last, she'd be able to walk and talk with her friends, without her mother listening in.

"Good. Now, you know the rules. I expect you to follow them at all times."

"I know, I know. You've told me before."

"Yes, I'm only reminding you because the well is not a safe place to linger on your own."

"Yes, I know, I know. Father says that women who linger there make themselves living prey, but that won't happen to me, Mama."

"Okay, you tell me the rules then."

"Always go with friends." Miriam counted them off on her fingers. "Always stay together. Never leave your friends alone and don't let them leave you."

"Good, now what do you do if something bad happens?"

"If someone is injured or too tired to keep up, one of us stays with her while the others go get help."

"Right and that's why—"

"We always travel in groups of four." Miriam finished for her mother.

"That's right. So, from tomorrow, there'll be no

sleeping in. You have to get up early and join the others. If you oversleep, it'll be too late, and we'll have no water for the day."

"Why can't I just go when I wake up then?"

"Well, firstly because it gets too hot and you'll struggle bringing the jug home in the heat. Secondly, no one goes to the well at that time of day, so you won't have anyone to walk with you and you only ever go in a group—"

"Of at least four. Yes, I know that."

"Good. Because only outcasts and undesirables go to the well during the heat of the day. I don't want you anywhere near them." Her mother warned.

"Don't worry Mama. There's Neriah, Sheerah, Mary and me. That's four. We'll be fine." Miriam slipped her hand inside her mother's and smiled. She did not see the sadness that lingered in the older woman's eyes.

The sun was up by the time they neared the well. Miriam and her mother greeted the other women and took up their places in line as the women waited for their turn to fill their jars. Other women smiled and greeted the pair.

Someone had filled the animal trough nearby and several donkeys were drinking from it. Those fortunate enough to have donkeys used them to do the heavy lifting. Full water jugs were tied to ropes slung over the animal's backs, which meant that these women could fetch much more water on a single trip. Miriam's family had never owned a donkey. Her father refused to buy one claiming that the beasts were stubborn and hard to manage, but Miriam suspected that the real reason was that he preferred to spend his money on himself.

They had reached the front of the queue and Miriam's mother lowered the earthen jug from her shoulder, placing it gently on the ground beside the well. When she straightened, Miriam saw her face was pale. Her mother stumbled slightly and caught hold of one of the wooden beams that supported the roof of the well.

"Why don't you sit a while, Mama. I'll draw the water."

Her mother did not argue. She sank down gratefully onto the dust on the shady side of the well, leaning her back against the cool stone.

Miriam began filling her jar with the crystal clear, cool water. She got to thinking about the age-old story of the well. It was a romantic story – the kind she liked best. In the story, one of the forefathers of the nation of Israel, a man named Jacob, had met his future wife Rachel right here at this very spot. Miriam could picture the scene in her mind – a dashing young man, a beautiful shepherdess, their love blossoming like the wild flowers after the rain, and all around them the orange and pink hues of the desert.

Jacob's mother Rebekah had always loved him more than his twin brother Esau, who had been born first and was their father's favourite. With his mother's help, Jacob had played a trick on his blind father by pretending to be Esau and stealing the first-born blessing that should have been bestowed on Esau.

Esau was furious and threatened to kill Jacob, so Rebekah sent Jacob to live with her cousin Laban until his brother's fury abated.

Jacob arrived at the well just as Rachel had come to water her sheep. Miriam pictured them speaking shyly to one another; Jacob discovering that Laban – the very man he had been sent to find – was her father.

She was so beautiful that he instantly fell in love with her and decided he wanted to marry her. Jacob was obviously the sort of man who always got what he wanted. He clearly had a way of manipulating people and situations to his own end. Alas, he, who had tricked his brother out of his birth-right, became the victim of Laban's trickery. The old man orchestrated a switch so that after working for seven years, Jacob found Rachel's elder sister Leah behind the wedding veil. Poor Jacob had worked for seven years only to end up married to the wrong sister.

Miriam tried to imagine Jacob's shock when he finally discovered the truth. Naturally, Jacob had complained to Laban, who only responded that it was customary to marry the elder sister off first. He conceded that Jacob could have both sisters, but he would have to work another seven years to marry Rachel.

Miriam could not decide whether she admired Jacob or not. A manipulator who finally had the tables turned on him at a heavy cost. Regardless, he rose to the challenge and eventually married Rachel and became one of the founding fathers of the faith. Jacob's son Joseph fathered Ephraim and Manasseh from whom the entire

Samaritan tribe descended. The well had been named to honour Jacob, and as the story went, he and his wives had lived here for many happy years.

One of the most fascinating aspects of the story for Miriam was that Rachel was a shepherdess. Imagine that – the mother of the nation being a lowly shepherdess.

In these more modern times, it was not considered fitting for someone of Miriam's social class to herd sheep. The villagers all looked down on the shepherds and farmhands as they belonged to a lower caste, but Miriam envied them. She thought of Rachel out there amongst the hills, tending her father's flock, and yearned to have that same freedom. Village women of Miriam's class were relegated to the home, family and duty. Her lot in life was to be a good wife, take care of the household chores and raise children.

How she wished she had lived in the times of Jacob and Rachel, when she might have tended to a little flock of sheep. She imagined that a shepherd's life would be carefree, without the rules and obligations that bound her life in the village. The world must have been a simpler place back then.

"Miriam." Her mother's hand on her shoulder snapped Miriam out of her daydream. "Are you almost finished my dear? You look like you're a million miles away."

"Oh, sorry Mama." She peered into the earthen vessel and saw that it was nearly full. "I'm almost done."

"Good, because we should be getting back. Let's see how you go carrying it all the way yourself today."

Miriam's mother placed a piece of rolled-up cloth on top of her head like a linen crown. She then helped Miriam to lift the heavy jar and balance it on the crown. Miriam held on to the jar with both hands as they made their way slowly down the path.

"It's a long walk home carrying this, Mama."

"Yes dear, but as you get stronger it will get easier." She smiled at Miriam and quietly added, "I'm proud of you, my girl. And I love you."

"I love you too, Mama."

Miriam felt buoyed by her mother's encouragement. Though the weight pressed heavy on her neck and small shoulders, she walked tall and straight. She vowed never to let her mother down.

Chapter III

Ancient Way

*Samaritans believe that theirs is the true religion
of the ancient Israelites, preserved by those who remained
in the Land of Israel after it had been conquered by the
Assyrians. They view Judaism as a religious practice
corrupted by the mingling of races during the Babylonian
exile.*

Ancient Way

Stand at the crossroads and look.
Ask for the ancient way.
Find the river that is laced with hope
Like a beautiful golden inlay.

Walk quiet and walk dignified
Peaceful as you go.
Look ahead to the truth,
And be content to take it slow.

Here upon the old roads
Where many have trod before,
Is the forging of your fortitude
Without the keeping score.

Here is the good path to walk upon.
Here is the good way to go.
Here you will know a quiet,
And find rest, for your soul.

Fear will fall away like dew
Evaporated in the sun.
One foot in front of the other now
As there is no need to run.

The heart will grow new muscle
And courage will take on form.
You will be found here standing,
At the dawn of every morn.

Salvation is here and now
For the Lord has heard your cry,
And from the dust of ancient heartache
You will walk out the miles.

Look towards the ancient trails.
Look for wisdom's way.
You already know where you're going
So let there be no more delay.

Miriam – age 15

iriam woke in the early hours of the morning with a word on her lips. *Artesian.* She had heard it in a dream. *Artesian spring.* The words were as clear as day, like birdsong that floated on the wind.

In the dream, she had seen a well full to overflowing with clean, pure water. Although she had never heard the word *artesian* before, in her dream the overflowing well had been called an *artesian spring*. It was nothing like the wells she knew from her home in the desert.

Jacob's well, outside of Sychar, was certainly deep, but exhausting to draw from. It took many pitchers to fill a jar. But oh – the well in her dream had bubbled up relentlessly and endlessly in streams of fresh clear water because it was connected to an underground source that never ran dry. A source that was pushed up from inside the earth's huge storage vaults by the pressure squeezing in from all sides. This pressure was so strong, it caused an endless flow that leapt forth like a miracle from the ground – difficult to comprehend and yet undeniable.

Miriam did not have vivid dreams often. She usually slept so deeply that, most nights, she did not remember her dreams at all. Now in the grey hours of morning she lay in her small bed holding onto the fading dream, going over the details in her mind. It felt significant and she wanted to remember it before the day's activity destroyed its clarity.

In the dream, Miriam had been standing by the well. She had been telling the people around her that there was a well that never ran dry; a well they could go to anytime they needed, and drink from so freely and deeply that they would never thirst again.

"Imagine being free of the daily hardship of drawing water," she told them. "The unrelenting need to fetch and carry water is exhausting. Come now to this artesian spring. It is here. Can you see its deeper meaning?"

Excitement lingered in her chest as she blinked and wiped the sleep from her eyes. *That word artesian. What did it really mean? Who could she ask? Who would understand? What was the deeper meaning she had been so excited to share in the dream?*

Unable to go back to sleep, she had watched the night turn from black to grey. The sparrows began singing about half an hour before dawn. *Was it the birds that roused the sun or the sun's arrival that roused the birds?* She couldn't be sure, but she liked to think that the sparrows called the sun forth from its hiding place, beckoning it to edge its way above the horizon until there was no stopping it. No more hesitation to begin the new day.

Every morning, Miriam would sneak out of the house to sit on the bench beside the front door. Hugging her knees tight, she would watch the sun appear. Today, as she sat there, breathing the cool morning air, thoughts of her dream returned.

The endless spring had been linked to some

incredible news that she had been eager to share. But now that she was awake, she could not recall what it was. *Did it have something to do with her faith?*

Miriam's people lived in hope that a Saviour would come – the Divine Leader foretold by the Holy Scriptures. Her mother spoke often of how much she longed to see the day when that Saviour arrived.

Over the years, Miriam had heard this wish expressed so often that she tended to tune it out. She was easily distracted and often resentful over the amount of work she was given to do, and hearing her mother speak lovingly of this Saviour while they laboured, did little to relieve her mood. But something in her dream reminded her of this prophecy. The dream had been so vivid and so beautiful it made her curious to know more. *Could the eternal well be a sign of His coming? Who could she ask?*

Certainly not her father. Although he was high up in the order of the Samaritan church and spent many hours studying the ancient Scriptures, she wondered if he actually believed in anything at all beyond himself. *He's such a hypocrite. He's fanatical about keeping all the rules that govern our lives, but he can't govern his own tongue.*

As far as Miriam could see, he was only interested in elevating his own status amongst the important leaders of Sychar. Whenever Miriam and her mother accompanied him into town for ceremonies, such as the Feast of Tabernacles, he put on a wonderful show, impressing everyone, charming them with his charisma and speaking kindly to all he met. He held lengthy conversations with anyone who would listen, as if he was a Rabbi. The duplicity in his behaviour made her resent him even more. How could he pretend to be so nice, when inside the confines of his home, his words ripped shreds off her heart?

She no longer hoped for his love and had given up the fruitless task of trying to please him. Her strategy had become one of surviving the day as unscathed as possible. She learnt to play games in her head to drown out the harsh words and let them slip away. Her mother had quietly instructed her to, "Let his words fall off you like water." But, as hard as she tried to become numb, to protect herself from his distain, the loathing that poured from him still hurt her deeply. So she took to avoiding him as much as possible. She rarely looked at him or spoke to him anymore.

Miriam wondered if she should ask her mother about the dream, but Mama was always so busy and so exhausted. She wasn't sure she should trouble her.

Unlike her friends, Miriam had no brothers or sisters, and therefore, she was her mother's sole help in running their household. It wasn't a large house, but they were comfortable and never went without. Miriam didn't know why she had no siblings and felt she could not ask her mother about it without being disrespectful, but she longed for a little brother or sister. The other families in town were so large and seemed full of life and joy. In comparison, Miriam felt like she lived inside an empty shell. On the surface her life looked shiny and polished, but inside it was hollow and cold.

The sun was above the horizon now. It was time to go in and prepare breakfast for her father before he left the house and before she began her commute to the well. Opening the door to the common area, which constituted kitchen and living space, she quietly pulled the flat bread from the shelf, added a small jar of olive oil and a few pieces of fruit to the plate. She filled a cup with water from the earthen jug and placed it all on a tray.

Her mother appeared in the doorway with a shawl wrapped around her shoulders. She sat down next to Miriam and smiled at her. Miriam wondered whether she should mention the dream.

"Good morning, my girl. Did you sleep well?"

Miriam nodded.

"That's good. Listen, I'm going to town with your father today. Do your chores, and when you're done, you can go for a walk if you like. Just be home in time to prepare the evening meal. We will try to be back before sunset."

Miriam nodded. She made up her mind to keep the dream to herself for now.

In the dim morning light, Miriam could see the remnants of her mother's once startling beauty. Her coal black eyes, exotic features and olive complexion belied her Assyrian heritage.

Miriam had inherited her mother's dark eyes and delicate features, but her skin was lighter. This came from her father. He was a Samaritan from the tribe of Manasseh and extremely proud of it.

He never ceased reminding Miriam and her mother of their mixed blood. According to him, the Samaritans were the only pure bloodline, and their way was the only *true* way. The Jews who had returned from captivity in Babylon had brought a corrupted version of the true faith back with them. Only the remnant left behind – true Samaritans like his ancestors, who had avoided captivity and kept themselves pure – had retained the original, unaltered version of the truth. He hung his pride on his heritage.

Though she had his complexion, Miriam had not inherited her father's religious zeal. She had been raised in the Samaritan tradition, but she lacked heartfelt conviction. She was obedient and went along to all the required religious festivals, keeping all the rules and regulations, but the truth that she didn't dare share with anyone, was that she didn't really know what she believed. All she really knew was that she wasn't as sure as her father was that his was the only true religion.

Once her parents had gone to town, Miriam hurried through her chores including a trip to the well. She could not wait to get out of the house and into the hills. Around mid-morning, she put a few pieces of bread and an apple into her shoulder bag, picked up her walking staff and headed out the door. With excitement drumming in her veins, she headed along the trail leading up to the flat rock that marked the entrance to the hill country.

She felt free here in the wilderness, away from the

town, the confines of society, and the duties that burdened her young life. Out in nature, her own faith truly came alive. She experienced peace in a way that she never felt inside four walls. *If only God would answer her many questions and prayers.*

When she reached the flat rock, she put her staff and bag down and stretched her arms above her head, letting the loose folds of her tunic fall away from her shoulders. It was a beautiful day. A gentle wind stirred the bushes and cooled her skin.

Which way then? She deliberately turned her back on Sychar and looked across to the distant hills. Spontaneously, she turned left, walking along the ridge. She knew the trails intimately, yet there was fresh exhilaration each time she walked them.

The path she had chosen ran down the hillside and into a grassy plain. Miriam ran across the plain with the wind at her back and a thrill in her heart. The brittle desert grass scraped at her legs and prickles clung to the hem of her tunic, but she didn't care. Out here, she did not need to worry about such things.

On the other side of the plain, she came to a small oasis – a magical place where she had often played as a young child. While it was usually a dry rocky hollow surrounded by shrivelled foliage, the scene altered completely after the rain. Run-off from the mountains turned the dusty grooves and the rocky indents into crystal-clear ponds and a stream that brought the vegetation beside it back to life.

Miriam sat down to wash her hands and face. The water was cool and refreshing as sunlight glinted off its surface. The pond reminded Miriam of her dream.

Suddenly, she sensed she wasn't alone and looked around. "Who is here?" No one answered.

Standing up, she wondered where the stream began and decided to follow it upwards into the hillside to find its source, something she had never done before. Perhaps there was a spring somewhere like the one in her dream.

The trail became steeper, and in some places, she had to climb around boulders where little waterfalls tumbled down over the rocks.

As she walked, Miriam spoke quietly to God – not in the way you would address an all-powerful leader, but in the way you would talk to a dear friend. Like a small child might chatter to its mother.

"Was that dream from You, God? What *is* an artesian spring? I want to understand. Please, help me to understand."

Miriam felt no fear as she climbed, only the excitement of discovery. Her eyes were open wide to the wonder of nature, and she saw God's creativity everywhere. She was lost in the wonder of it all.

She noticed the details. The tiny veins that ran along the underside of every leaf. The intricate petals on small grass flowers, and the softness of the velvet green moss on the rocks she passed by. Suddenly a group of butterflies flew up and surrounded her in a cloud of blue and yellow wings. She stood in awe and laughed aloud as they swarmed around her, some landing on her tunic.

The sound of the water rushing grew louder the higher she climbed. She imagined it was the roar of God's own voice. She felt closer than she ever had to the Creator. Here she could see His handy work. The way He wove it all together like her mother at her weaving loom, creating a masterpiece, stitch by careful stitch. *If God did this with His Creation, could He do the same with her life? Was it possible that the One who made the heavens also cared for her — small and insignificant as she was? Miriam barely dared to hope that it might be true.*

The God of the ancient teachings and daily rituals of religious duty, always seemed distant and difficult to understand. To Miriam he seemed cold, impersonal and aloof, much like her own father. The God her soul recognised out here in the wilderness felt different. This God, her God, took her breath away in moments of unspeakable joy. In his presence, instead of fear, she experienced a delight that words could not explain.

The trail ended at the base of a waterfall where water cascaded in a mighty, gushing freefall down a cliff face more than thirty feet above her. The sheer rock wall was wet and slippery with blooms of green-black algae. Miriam stood back in awe, letting the spray dapple her body. She lifted her arms to feel it on her skin. She took off her headscarf and placed it in the crook of a tree. Then she cupped her hands beneath a rivulet of cold water. She poured the water over her head, smoothing it over her long dark hair. Then she breathed deeply, taking huge lungfuls of the moist clean air.

"If only this was closer to home," she whispered. "This would be much more exciting than going to the old well for water every day." But then, she reasoned, if it was closer, she wouldn't have this wonder all to herself. Miriam decided she was thankful for the long trek that kept others away.

She wondered if any other women from the town ever escaped their chores long enough to find their own secret places. She knew none of her friends wandered in the wild as she did. Even when they did have time, they were not inclined to leave the safety of town.

Miriam made herself comfortable on the rocks beside the falls, closed her eyes and allowed her thoughts to wander. It did not take long for her mind to return to her dream. This place was nothing like the well she had seen in the dream, but it was strange to her that she had come across this seemingly endless flow of water on the day after having a dream about an endlessly flowing well.

"Miriam?" The voice roused her and sent her heart racing. She sat up and looked around.

"Oh. Michael, you shouldn't see me like this. Turn your back." He did as she instructed. She jumped up and hurriedly put on her headscarf.

"Okay," she said sheepishly when she had reestablished order. "You can turn around now."

As he turned to face her, she noticed that his dark

eyes were smiling. His own hair lay in the usual unruly mess of curls on top of his head. She also noted that he had grown a beard. It changed his boyish features into those of a man, and she felt a little afraid. Social norms had kept them apart, and they had not spoken to each other since the day of the storm all those years ago.

"Sorry. I didn't mean to scare you. I saw someone wandering up here and I was curious. What are you doing here all by yourself, little sis?" His old nickname for her made her smile. She relaxed, silently scolding herself for even questioning her safety – it was only Michael the shepherd; Michael who always gave a friendly wave whenever they passed by at a distance.

Heat filled her cheeks – had he seen her dance and jump along the trail in wild abandon? "I was just walking," she replied. "I like exploring. What are *you* doing here?"

"Oh, I always come here after the rains." He sat down a respectful distance from her. "It's one of my favourite places." He hesitated. "You really shouldn't be here alone though. What if you had slipped and fallen, and I wasn't here to rescue you?" A cheeky grin lit up his face.

"And why is it ok for *you* to be out here alone then? What if *you* fell and *I* wasn't here to rescue you?"

He laughed at her quick response and shrugged his shoulders. "*I* don't have a choice."

"Well, I'm fine. I love being out in the hills."

"I know you do. I often see you out here. No one else wanders the hills like you do – apart from the shepherds that is."

"There's no better place to be."

"If you don't mind me asking, what are you running away from, little sis?"

"Nothing. I'm not running away. I just like being out here. *Alone*."

"Oh. Is that a hint?" He said, preparing to boost himself off the rock.

He was going to leave. She searched in vain for something to say that would make him stay without compromising her position in the argument.

"You know," said Michael, dusting his hands off on the back of his tunic. "If you stand with your back flat up against the rocks and look out from behind the edge of the waterfall, the sun casts a beautiful rainbow through the spray. Do you want to see it?"

A rainbow. Miriam nodded eagerly. She loved rainbows, and they were a rare sight in Sychar. "Here, let me show you." He held out a hand to help her up.

Together they picked their way over to the cliff face. Miriam admired the ease with which his sandaled feet moved over the rocky ground. She longed to be as strong and agile as he was, to live as he did in the hills and go anywhere she pleased with no pressure and no one telling her what to do.

"Come on." He shuffled along a narrow ledge with his back pressed against the cliff wall. The water thundered down right beside him. "You can see the rainbow from here."

Gathering her courage, she made her way towards him.

"Stand like this," he instructed, squaring his shoulders against the cliff with his back up against the wall. He was a good two feet taller than her, and though she was a woman now and not the little girl he had once carried on his back, she felt like a small child standing beside him.

He pointed upwards into the falling cascade of water. She turned her eyes and looked up, although squinting to protect them from the spray. Her heart skipped a beat. Reaching out from the centre of the flow was a brilliant arc of multiple colours. It stretched out into thin air and disappeared as if held up by an unseen hand.

"It's beautiful."

"Yes," said Michael. "One of the most beautiful things I've ever seen." She turned towards him to find that he had transferred his gaze from the rainbow and was staring into her upturned face.

Michael's hand gently moved a rebellious curl from the side of her face, tucking it back into place beneath her scarf. Their eyes locked, and Miriam felt lightheaded. No one except her mother had ever told her she was beautiful. His candour, the intensity of his gaze and the proximity of his body, just inches away from hers, frightened her. She felt a sudden urge to flee. She pushed herself away from the wall and hurried back to the rock. She picked up her bag and staff.

"I better go now. It's getting late, and I've got dinner to prepare for my parents."

"Let me walk down with you. It's almost time to take the sheep to the well and get them watered."

"Umm ... I don't—" Miriam was about to decline his offer, but he was at her side before she could complete her protest. Her father would tear strips off her if he knew she was up in the hills alone with a shepherd boy. The shame of it. She would never be allowed out of her house again. But despite the risk, Michael's presence felt reassuring, and she wanted to spend more time in his company. Unlike her father, Michael made her feel safe – mostly. She liked the way his eyes smiled at her and the cheekiness of his grin.

They walked in companionable silence until they came to the walled pasture on the outskirts of Sychar where Michael's sheep were grazing. He leaned against the stone wall and whistled, and they all came to him, gathering around like children. Miriam couldn't help but laugh at the way they baaed. He touched each one on the head and spoke affectionately to them. She could see the kindness in the way he treated them. The sheep trusted him completely. She wondered whether she would ever be able to trust a man that way.

Her belly growled loudly, reminding her that she had not eaten anything since breakfast. She removed the loaves of bread from her bag and offered one to Michael. He took it with thanks.

"Let's sit for a minute while we eat." He indicated a rocky mound. Taking her hand, Michael helped her climb up onto it and then nimbly jumped up himself.

"What's it like being a shepherd?" Miriam asked. "You seem to have such a free and easy existence. I've always envied you."

"Oh, I'm happy enough, but I don't think you should envy me. My parents died when I was very young so, I came to Sychar to live with my uncle. These are his sheep. I tend them for him in compensation for my place at his table. Although, I eat and sleep with the sheep." He smiled wryly.

"I was only about seven years old when I arrived. I remember being very afraid, but I was thankful to have food in my belly. The other shepherds taught me how to care for the sheep and how to defend them against wild animals." Miriam's eyes widened though she tried not to show the fear she felt at the thought of fighting off wild animals.

"You're right, though," he continued. "There is freedom being out in the open with only the sheep for company. But there is also danger and great responsibility. My uncle values his sheep highly and hands out severe punishments to any shepherd who lets harm come to them. So, I spend almost all my time watching over my sheep. I never leave them except for short periods and then only if they're in a walled pasture like this one or in the barn closer to town."

"I hardly ever see my uncle and his family – except on holy days when we make our pilgrimage to the temple. Over the years, the sheep have become my family, and the way I see it, we look after each other. I understand how you feel about the hills too. I miss them whenever I'm away from them, but believe me, my life is far from easy. And," he added as an afterthought, "it can be lonely."

"I still envy you," she sighed. "I would fight off wild animals and sleep in a barn with sheep if it meant I had the freedom to roam the hills instead of being trapped in our house all day. Home feels like prison to me. The only time I ever get out is to go to the well in the mornings with the other women."

"Have you ever thought that perhaps anywhere can feel like prison if you're locked up on the inside?" Michael probed gently. Miriam frowned.

"I don't know what you mean?"

"Well, take me for instance. You say you envy my freedom to roam around the hills. I'm saying the freedom you truly crave runs deeper than that. It's a spiritual freedom, and it doesn't come from being able to spend my days in the hills. Even out here, I could still be a prisoner. I know many unhappy shepherds who don't feel free." He waved a hand towards the hillside.

"But how could you possibly be trapped when you have so much space?"

"I'm talking about being trapped on the inside. You see, if I lived in fear, resentment or unforgiveness, I'd be just as much a captive as if I were behind steel bars."

"So, how did you get your inside freedom?"

"The sheep helped me find freedom from the prison

inside my own heart. They taught me kindness, humility and unconditional love. They helped me to get over my grief, to forgive my parents for leaving me all alone, and to understand many things that I couldn't understsand when I was younger. I think it is this freedom you see in me, and this freedom you seek for yourself. I won't lie to you, though. These lessons did not come easily or quickly, they came at a cost, but I am thankful for them."

Miriam squirmed. Although she sensed the truth in his words, she cared nothing for the suffering they implied. She preferred to think of his life as wonderful and carefree. Her life on the other hand was filled with duty and obligation.

"But you don't know what it's like to live in my house," she said and winced at how petulant this sounded even to her own ears.

"Oh, I know your father a little." Michael picked at a patch of moss beside his thigh.

Miriam looked up in surprise. "You do?"

"Yes. He is a distant relative of my uncle. An ancestor on his – well, your – side of the family was chosen to be a scribe by the priests, and your ancestors moved up the social ladder. They are ashamed of us. They don't want anyone to know they come from a family of lowly farmers and shepherds. Your father won't even greet us in the street. But I've watched how he behaves, all gallant and charming, and I can't help thinking it's all a ruse."

Miriam gaped at him. She'd had no idea that Michael was a distant relative. And even more amazing was how Michael had seen through her father's posturing in a way that most people had never seemed able to.

"How have you seen anything of my father? You live in the hills."

"I return for the holy days, remember? I've seen enough over the years. Heard enough from my uncle too."

Suddenly, she wanted to drop the subject of her father. "I should go now," she blurted.

"Yes." That intense stare pinned her to the spot once more. Then the spell broke, he leapt from the mound and helped her down. "That's probably wise. I've got to get these sheep watered."

Still a little miffed by their conversation, Miriam avoided his outstretched hand and jumped down from the mound.

A muddle of feelings swirled around inside her – a mixture of indignation, shame and a strange wonder that she'd never felt before. It frightened her, and she had a sudden urge to get as far away from Michael as she possibly could. "Goodbye, Michael," she said before quickly turning to hurry down the trail.

She didn't see the look in his eyes as he watched her go.

Chapter IV

Missing

In Samaritan tradition when a person dies, male relatives able to read the Book of the Holy Law are commissioned to stay with the body. During their vigil, they read the whole Law from beginning to end.

You are everywhere
And nowhere,
Which makes it the worst kind of missing.
The unbearable constant reminders
That you were here
Just a moment ago.
And that minute will stretch itself
Into hours and days
Then weeks and months.
Endless reminders
And a constant underpin,
Telling me again and again
That you are everywhere
And nowhere
That is close enough for me to hold.
So, I won't look too far forward.
I'll try to stay right here
In this quiet,
And be ok with the lack
And the wait
And the absence,
Because they do say that a heart that has lost
Is a heart that has loved.
Don't they?
I'll pull it in and twist it up tight
Like it's a ball of twine,
Over and over
One bit at a time,
Until my big knot of missing you
Is something else entirely.
But what it becomes
I can't yet be sure of.
Let's just wait and see.

Miriam – age 17

iriam sat on the edge of her mother's bedside. She had hardly moved in hours. Crushed by the weight of her grief, she could barely breathe. In her mind, the same anthem played, stuck on repeat.

How can this be happening? I prayed. We believed. Why did God not listen? I believed. Why did God not care?

It had been two years since the day she had met Michael by the waterfall. She had not known then, but her mother had gone into town that day to seek healing from the priests at the temple. She had continued to do so until she was too weak to walk. They had anointed her with holy oil and prayed that her weakness and pain would disappear. Her father had given them money to make sacrifices on her behalf. God Almighty had been made aware of her plight. His help fervently requested. But none had been forthcoming.

As she sat by her mother's bedside with nothing left to offer, no prayer left to pray, Miriam lamented that it had all been in vain. Nothing they had done had made the least bit of difference. Despite their best efforts, her beautiful mother lay dying, and there was nothing that anyone could do about it.

Hopelessness heavy as summer rain fell into all of the cracks and crevices of Miriam's soul. *How could she live without her mother? How would she go on?* She felt lost and so terribly alone. She had never stood one day upon the earth without her mother by her side. *Constant. Unconditional. Faithful. There. Always there.*

Broken and aching, Miriam sobbed, letting her tears fall freely, unable to hold them in. An endless, pointless heart's cry, "Oh no. No, please God. No." In her mind, she could see her mother, still young, vibrant and full of life.

She had been so wonderfully kind too. Despite her father's protests, Mama had befriended the outcasts and looked after the old and frail. Whenever she baked bread, she always doubled the recipe and made a loaf for a neighbour or someone in need. She even fed the stray dogs that wandered about the town.

Miriam had trailed after her through the streets of Sychar delivering supplies to those in need. In private moments with her daughter, when she let down her guard, her sense of fun and humour, would have them both in fits of laughter. All these treasured memories of her mother only made Miriam miss her more than ever.

Never before had Miriam felt such sadness and anger all at once. As much as she was sad to lose her mother, she felt anger towards her for leaving her, and towards God who had ignored all their pleas to save this woman who had served him so faithfully. She could not fathom how her mother kept up her faith in a God who refused to help her. Despite the mysterious nature and unhalting progression of her illness, Miriam's mother had called her over and whispered words that left her reeling.

"I'm thankful for this illness, Miriam. It has allowed

me to see a side of your father that I have never seen before. He has been so kind. He has looked after me so well and been so attentive. I am thankful."

At first, Miriam had not believed him capable of any form of kindness that was not a manipulation tactic – a ploy to get his own way. But as she watched him caring for her mother, she saw that he *was* capable of it after all. He had simply never bothered to show her this kindness while she was healthy and vital.

Her mother might be grateful for it, but it made Miriam furious. She could not believe how much his kindness touched her mother's soul. It riled her to think that her mother had to be at death's door before her father showed her any true kindness. *Why had he taken so long to show compassion?* Was it only the thought of losing his wife that goaded him into action? By the time he decided to treat her as she deserved, it was almost too late.

Her mother's next words almost stopped Miriam's heart from beating. "It's okay, my darling. God's ways are not our ways. Though we have prayed for healing, now I'm looking forward to the end."

Looking forward to the end? Miriam could not believe her ears. She didn't want her mother to let go. She wanted her to fight. She needed her to fight. But instead, her mother lay there in complete surrender, letting her life slip away and, worst of all, claiming that she was happy about it. *Did she not care who she was leaving behind? Did she not give a thought to those who would be lost without her? Was she just so tired that she no longer cared about anything?*

These intrusive and hurtful thoughts played on repeat as Miriam allowed her emotions to overwhelm her. While her mother slept, Miriam silently begged her to recover – to find the will to fight this awful disease and return to her. Behind her the bedroom door opened quietly, and her father entered the room, a priest trailing behind him like a shadow.

"Miriam, stop that at once," her father snapped. "Crying will only upset your mother."

The priest's head jerked up at the harsh tone but he did not utter a word. Hiding his surprise, he hurried over to the bed. Miriam's mother stirred and moaned in her sleep. "It's okay, my dear," the priest soothed. Then turning to Miriam's father, he added, "I don't expect it will be long now."

"What?" Miriam blurted. "What are you saying?"

"Miriam, stop that. If you can't control yourself, you'd better get—"

The priest raised his hand. Her father stopped midsentence. Miriam gaped. She had never seen anyone silence her father before.

"She doesn't have long," he repeated. "It's time to say your goodbyes."

Miriam could not get breath past the lump of pain in her throat. *How could this be happening?* The priest placed a folded towel on her mother's forehead and wiped the cold sweat away from her brow. Her shallow, irregular breathing seemed to fill the room. The priest stood beside her head and began the death ritual, reciting the final Song of Moses from beginning to end. The melancholy drone of Scripture filled the air while desperate thoughts raced through Miriam's mind. *No Mama. Oh Mama, I love you.* She turned to her father. The priest's words had shifted him into stillness. He stood stunned and unmoving like a stone statue on the far side of the room.

When the priest had completed the recital, he proceeded with the formal confession of faith, repeating it three times. Miriam crouched beside her mother. She held her mother's hand tightly and laid her head gently on her chest, letting relief flood through her every time that birdlike chest expanded beneath her cheek. Her father, still silent, moved closer now. It seemed he had finally run out of fight. His big hands clasped together in front of him, and his head bowed low. He appeared to be listening intently to each word the priest uttered.

Miriam tried to ignore the presence of both men – only her mother mattered.

"We confess this on her behalf, O' Lord, for she has confessed it many times." The priest's words drifted and hovered over them. "My belief is in You, O' Lord, and in Moses, the son of Amram your servant, and in Mount Gerizim Bethel, and in the Holy Law, which is the fairest thing on earth. There is no God but One. Moreover, I bear witness to the Day of Requital and Reward. True it is forever: there is no God but One. By Him we live, and by Him we die and by Him we shall be raised up. All who repent and all who love You are in Thy Holy Keeping, O' Lord God."

In that moment, her mother's breathing stopped. Miriam waited and held her breath. Willed her mother to keep going. Pleaded with her. "Mama, no. I need you. You can't be gone." She listened as hard as she could, but could hear no soft inhalation, could feel no rise and fall of her chest. Though no amount of denial could change the situation, she simply could not allow herself to face the truth. She clutched her mother's face in both her hands and was shocked to find it altered in a way that she hadn't expected. It was the same beloved face, but it lacked something. Her mother wasn't there. Miriam was filled with a deep and almost tangible knowledge that although her body was still present, her mother's spirit had departed. Denial gave way to sorrow, and her mother's passing felt like a thick blanket of heavy fog that threatened to suffocate her.

The priest began to recite hymns of praise and assurance that her mother would enter the Garden of Eden on the Day of Requital and Reward. While his words rose and fell around her, grief dragged a dagger through her broken heart. The pain was so sharp and intolerable she thought she might rip right open.

"Grandeur is pertained for the Lord, the Great King, for all His ways are judgment: a God of truth and without perversity."

Miriam's eyes blurred with tears as she looked at her mother's face, so beautiful and peaceful in the light.

"He is the Master of the Kingdom and His Dominion is over all its generations. His is the Mighty Hand. Tremendous is He in praise, performing wonders."

She gritted her teeth and tried not to scream. *Where were his healing wonders? Where was God's power to restore? Did it even exist?*

"There is no God but One. He alone abides and continues for ever and holds the life everlasting. Whatever exists apart from him at some time passes away and is lost, but he does not pass away and is not lost. In his hands are all things. He giveth death and he giveth life."

Her father approached and she felt his hand upon her shoulder. She realised that he too was weeping for the loss of his wife, and perhaps also for the regrets he now carried. Miriam shrank way from his touch. She was angry with her father. He didn't deserve to weep. She would not comfort the man who had inflicted so much pain upon the woman he was supposed to love.

"He sustains all things. He judges and he heals, and there is no escape from his hands. Therefore, it is for all mortal men to observe the commandments of the Lord, the Ever-Existent God. For so shall there be unto them a path whereby they may reach their goal, to behold the face of their Master. And all their works shall be held in good liking, and when they die, their Master shall show favour unto them. Happy is he who dies in the faith of Moses the prophet."

Happy? Miriam's anger flared once more. *What good*

were these empty rituals in the face of her pain? They had brought no healing to her mother and offered no comfort to her now.

She got up and turned towards the door, locking eyes with her father as she did so. Though her mind raced at a thousand miles a minute and her heart hammered hard against her chest, she stared at him silently as tears streamed down her cheeks, unable to find the words to describe the bitter resentment she felt towards him. She turned back to her mother, bent over and kissed her forehead.

"Goodbye my sweet Mama." Tears blurred her vision as she ran from the room, through the courtyard and out into the street.

Miriam ran through the busy marketplace where, to her utter amazement, life appeared to be going on as normal. *How could this be when her mother had just died?* She wanted to scream at them, to demand that they stop what they were doing and join in her sorrow. She wanted to make them understand the gravity of what she had lost, but she didn't quite understand it herself. Her mother. The woman who birthed her and who had been there for her every single day of her life. The one who had taught her to bake and weave masterpieces and run a household. The one in whom she had found solace when her father's words had cut too deep. They had always depended on one another, and now she was gone. Miriam was alone. Nothing felt real. Nothing felt fair. *Where was God and why didn't He care? Why had God allowed this to happen?*

Miriam desperately wanted to believe that God cared. She had tried to be strong in the faith like her mother had been, but this loss left her undone. *Perhaps God – if he existed at all – was not loving as her mother had believed? If he could let a good woman like Mama die for no reason and way before her time, it seemed more likely that he was cold and uncaring – just like her father? Or maybe, God was too holy to bother? Afterall, why would a great and powerful God care about a girl such as Miriam? Then again, perhaps she was being punished. After all, she had a strong streak of rebellion in her. She wasn't interested in holy rituals. She just wanted to run into the wild and be free from the responsibilities of life. Was God punishing her by taking her mother away?*

These thoughts churned through her head as she ran on, out of town and up into the hills, trusting her feet to take her to her sanctuary. She wanted to be far away from her friends and relatives. Talking to anyone about the turmoil she felt inside might break her into pieces. When she reached the flat rock, she looked around to make sure she was alone. She did not want even Michael's company now. Certain of her solitude she unleashed the flood of emotions that threatened to overwhelm her. Miriam lay down on the rock and just let it all flow out.

Miriam had cried many times before, but she had never cried like she was crying now. Her grief felt like a bottomless pit inside her. Sorrow tumbled over like waves in a storm – one giant wall of water crashed over her, followed by another and another. She had no time to catch her breath. She felt sure she would drown in her grief and was powerless to stop it. It was terrifying.

Without her mother, she could see only darkness ahead of her and she didn't know how to find her way through it. She couldn't even see where her next step might land.

Evening slowly turned into night. The darkness inside her seemed to have leaked out, staining the landscape. The moon rose, casting its gentle light on rocks, bushes and sand. Far below candles glowed in windows. Miriam did not move or even contemplate returning home. She could not enter the house again and could not face her father. Instead, wrapped in her tunic and shawl, she curled up on the rock like a small child in a basket, feeling the cool in the night air and enjoying the dull pain as the rock's hard edges pressed into her bones. She continued to sob quietly until exhaustion overtook her and she fell sleep.

In the wind-still night, a thick layer of fog swept across the ground, covering her like a shroud. As she slept, her restless mind was troubled by frightening dreams. She wanted to surface from sleep to escape the torment, but fatigue and grief dragged her down at each attempt, and she did not wake until the early hours of the morning.

When she opened her eyes in the light of dawn, her face felt swollen and bruised, her limbs were stiff and her back ached from a night spent on the cold rock. For a moment, she was completely disorientated. Then it all came flooding back. She recalled her mother lying dead in her bed, face towards the sky, eyes closed, her skin cold and grey.

Miriam rolled over and tried to sit up, cradling her head in her hands as she did so. The birdsong she usually loved so dearly felt like cymbals clashing inside her skull. She wished that they would stop. She wished it would all go away.

"Mama," she whispered as the tears began to slide silently over her cheeks once more. Her tears seemed to flow from an endless spring that she knew would never run dry – a well of grief so deep and full of pain that it felt completely bottomless. Overwhelmingly deep. She had no idea how to hold back the waters of her sorrow, certain that they were so powerful as to simply go over, around and through anything that got in their way.

Thoughts of the endless spring brought back memories of the strange dream she'd had two years before. It had been so vivid as to become etched into her memory. From time to time over the years, she had pondered its meaning. She had been certain the well was filled with hope, but now that idea seemed impossibly naïve. She scoffed at its utter implausibility. Then a dire thought struck her. What if the water from the well was not hope at all, but sorrow.

It's an endless well of grief that will never leave me alone. Shaking her head to clear away this thought, she tried to stand. Her stiff legs caused her to stumble towards the edge of the rock. The sight of the sheer drop to the valley below caused another dark thought to surface. She could so easily end her own pain. She could join her mother and be done with this life. Miriam staggered closer to the edge. A whirlwind of thoughts danced through her brain.

Your pain will be over.

You don't have to endure this grief.

But this is not the way. Only a coward would do this.

No one will miss you or even care.

Your father would probably be happy.

Free from the responsibility of you.

There is nothing for you here. Just a life of servitude.

You want freedom. Here it is. Take it. It's so close.

Your mother would not want this. If she knew, she would be devastated.

It was the final thought that forced her to step away from the ledge. The absolute certainty that her mother would be horrified at such a decision was enough to sway her. Miriam hung her head in hopeless surrender. *So, what now?* Again, there was no answer – just the wind and an aching silence.

Finally, she made her way back to town, scrambling on unsteady feet down the steep embankment. She plodded along the trail that eventually forked around Sychar. Miriam wasn't sure where she would go, but she knew she could not and would not go home. There was no way she could face seeing her mother's lifeless body laid out and ready for burial. So, she took the path that led away from her own house.

Walking through the quiet streets in the dawn light, Miriam eventually stopped in front of Mary's house. She knew her friend would soon be waking and getting ready for her morning walk to the well.

She stood beneath the window and called softly, "Mary."

Nothing. She called again.

A face appeared at the window. Mary's eyes widened when she saw Miriam's swollen and dirty face.

"Miriam? What's the matter? You look terrible."

"Can I come in?" Her voice was hoarse and shaky as the tidal wave of grief threatened to wash over her again in the face of her friend's concern.

"Of course." Mary went to open the door.

Once inside, Miriam collapsed into Mary's arms.

"What is it, Miriam? What's happened?"

"Mama." Miriam began sobbing again. She didn't know how to gather up the floodwaters and make them stop. Her eyes were now so swollen she could barely open them, so she didn't even try. She could speak no further, but she knew Mary would understand. Not saying a word, Mary wrapped her arms around Miriam like a protective shield. She didn't tell her to stop crying. She just held her close, as if she were attempting to hold Miriam's soul together as she sobbed.

For the first time since her mother died, Miriam felt hands of comfort that reached deeper than the surface into her aching soul. Mary cried with her friend. Still wrapped in each other's arms they sank down onto a bench beside the smouldering fireplace in the courtyard of Mary's home.

The two young women stayed there for a long time. Every so often, Mary stroked the damp curls that poked out of Miriam's scarf trying fruitlessly to tuck them back in. Miriam did not notice Mary's mother approaching nor did she see the look that passed between the two women. Mary's mother wordlessly placed a cup of cool water, a blanket, and a pillow beside the pair on the bench. She nodded to Mary as she quietly retreated, leaving them alone once more.

Eventually, Mary let Miriam's head fall into her lap. Once her friend was sound asleep, she shifted away and, cupping Miriam's head in her hands, placed it gently on the pillow. Then she covered her with the blanket.

"Rest now my friend. There is water here if you're thirsty. I will prepare some food for you." She headed to the storeroom to find the makings of the morning meal.

Though Miriam slept, she was troubled by repetitive vivid and troubling dreams, and when she woke several hours later, she could not figure out where she was. *Why was she not on her sleeping mat?* The courtyard looked familiar, but this was not home. A cool light shone down on her and reflected on the whitewashed walls. Then it all came back to her. She thought of her mother and felt the hot heavy lump in her chest. She wondered where Mary was. *How long had she been asleep?*

She looked about and noticed the cup of water, and beside it, a small plate of bread and some fruit. Though her tummy grumbled at the sight of food, she couldn't face it.

The courtyard was deserted. She stared up at the sky and listened for sounds of life from the rest of the house. She thought she could hear voices nearby. Though she strained her ears, she could not make out the words. However, she could discern a back-and-forth nature to the exchange that made her wonder if they were arguing. Perhaps her presence in Mary's home was an unwelcome intrusion.

She had better leave, but where was she to go? Miriam sat in an agony of indecision. Her throat felt dry and dusty like the desert around Sychar. She gulped the water from the cup, drained it to its dregs, and wished for more. The aching in her head subsided somewhat. She picked up a piece of bread and nibbled at the corner, but the taste of food made her nauseous, so she returned it to the plate.

"Miriam?" Mary peered from the doorway of the adjacent room. "You're awake. That's good." She joined Miriam on the bench.

"How long did I sleep?"

"Several hours. It's almost midday now."

"Oh. I'm sorry. I didn't mean to intrude like that."

Mary held up her hand in protest. "No, it's completely fine. I'm glad you slept. You needed the rest." She hesitated before continuing. "But Miriam, we had to tell your father where you were. He had organised a search party—"

"My father? Is he angry?" Miriam cut in. She felt panic rise within her in anticipation of his anger but quashed it and focused her efforts on fortifying the stonewall she had built around her heart.

"He was at first. But he's been outside talking to my father for a while now, and I'd say he's calmed down quite a bit. He was worried when you didn't come home last night."

"I didn't plan to stay out all night, if that's what he's thinking—"

"I don't know what he's thinking, Miriam. Only that he had no idea where you were, and he was probably imagining the worst. It was a shock for him, on top of already losing your mother yesterday. I know you don't get along, but he's all you have now. Perhaps you should try to be a little understanding? My father would go crazy too if I was out all night." Mary's attempt to show her friend a new perspective only made Miriam more defensive.

"I didn't mean to. I just fell asleep outside. Up on the ridge. On the big flat rock."

"You slept there all night? By yourself?" Mary's eyes widened in shock.

"Yes."

"Miriam, you should have come here. Anything could have happened to you."

Miriam sighed. "Yes, perhaps I should have. I wasn't really thinking. I only knew that I didn't want to go home, Mary – not then and not now. And it's not just because of my mother either. Although, I really don't know how to live there, or anywhere, without her. It's my father. He's been planning my betrothal, and Mary, I don't want to marry. I don't want to get trapped like my mother was."

Miriam had never been so open with her friend before. Over the past few months, her parents had spoken to her about their plans for her betrothal to her second cousin Caleb, and despite her objections, the wheels had been set in motion.

While her mother was still alive, she had tried to convince Miriam that the match was a good one. Miriam had argued with her about it often. *Had the stress she created through her stubborn refusal advanced her mother's illness? Was she to blame for her death?*

Mary stared at her feet intently as if they were going to give her an answer. She was silent for a long time.

"I do understand. Believe me. Marriage scares me too. But Miriam, it might not be so bad for you. It will give you freedom from your father. Everyone in town knows how hard he is on you. Don't you want to escape and have a life of your own? Maybe have children one day? Just think, you can have your own house and family, and you won't have to see your father every day. You've said your cousin seems to be a nice man. Living with him will hopefully be better than life with your father."

Miriam was shocked that her friend spoke so candidly. *Did everyone really know how badly her father treated them?* Mary read her mind.

"Miriam, it's always been obvious. Also, our mothers are – were – good friends. I overheard your mother sharing her hardships with mine. I also heard her sharing her concern for your wellbeing after she had passed on, and her hope that your marriage would be a good one."

Miriam thought about her mother and the many arguments they had over the betrothal. She sighed, knowing full well that Mary spoke the truth.

"Yes, my mother wanted me to marry, and I hurt her deeply by refusing. I know that." Tears edged their way back into her eyes. "And yes, he's not bad. But don't you see? I don't want to be married to anyone."

"But Miriam, you don't really have a choice. We must marry someday. That's just the way things are."

"I know." A deep sense of resignation settled within Miriam's heart. No matter how much she fought against it, this was the path set out for her, the one she would have to walk. She could make it easy or hard, but she would walk it regardless.

She looked at Mary and her tears began to flow. Mary took Miriam's hands in both of her own and squeezed tight.

"No matter what, we will always be friends. I love you like you are one of my own sisters. Nothing can change that."

Miriam lay her head on her friend's shoulder and wept.

Chapter V

Hope Shines Brightest

Job 28:1-11 (NIV)

There is a mine for silver
and a place where gold is refined.
2 Iron is taken from the earth,
and copper is smelted from ore.
3 Mortals put an end to the darkness;
they search out the farthest recesses
for ore in the blackest darkness.
4 Far from human dwellings they cut a shaft,
in places untouched by human feet;
far from other people they dangle and sway.
5 The earth, from which food comes,
is transformed below as by fire;
6 lapis lazuli comes from its rocks,
and its dust contains nuggets of gold.
7 No bird of prey knows that hidden path,
no falcon's eye has seen it.
8 Proud beasts do not set foot on it,
and no lion prowls there.

[9] People assault the flinty rock with their hands
and lay bare the roots of the mountains.
[10] They tunnel through the rock;
their eyes see all its treasures.
[11] They search the sources of the rivers
and bring hidden things to light.

Hope shines brightest under fire
And burns hot within the rain.

It lets you glimpse its power
When it seems, there is no hope for change.

It is a force unlike any other
Stronger than your fear.

Hope will lead you through the valley
And out into the clear.

Hope is like a beacon
Standing high upon a distant hill.

Defiant through the night
As it tenaciously shines brighter still.

It will not ever be put to rest
And will not be diminished.

Hope is like the breath in you
Unending until the finish.

Deny its power all you want
But still, it won't be moved.

Hope has a stubborn nature
That will illuminate the path you choose.

It will suffer violence
But rise and rise, to stand again.

For hope has countless lives
And will never know an end.

Miriam – age 18

Although days sometimes felt endless, the year following her mother's death passed quickly. Miriam regularly resisted and fought against her father's plans for her betrothal, and when they were not arguing, they avoided one another. The truth was that she hated the confrontations with her father. They compounded her loneliness and grief. The seed of bitterness and resentment deep within Miriam's heart started to grow roots beyond her control. The walls of protection around her heart were high. He couldn't have reached her even if he'd tried. Not that he ever did. Her father was as absent and cold towards her as he had always been.

Miriam did attempt to be dutiful and diligent in her home tasks, completing her chores as competently and quickly as she could. And when they were finished, she went walking. Sometimes, Mary walked with her, and they talked; at other times, she went alone. On a few occasions, Michael found her. Or was it she who found him?

Out in the wild, another seed began to take root in her heart. Though unintentional, its roots also grew quickly. A small infatuation with Michael turned into something else entirely – something she had never experienced before. It sprang up like a weed – restless and untamed, and, although she refused to admit its existence, it began to take over every available lonely space.

Mary occasionally joined Miriam on her walks now and had noticed that Michael sometimes watched them from a distance. One day, as she and Miriam strode out across a field of brittle yellow grass, she asked, "Do you know that man?" Mary pointed to where Michael stood beneath a thorn tree some way off.

Miriam had not noticed him standing there. Her heart quickened at the sight of him. He was now ever taller and broad shouldered, with messy dark curls that framed his unshaven face. He smiled and waved when he saw her looking at him. His dark eyes shone, intense and mysterious, even from a distance.

She raised her hand to acknowledge him before quickly turning away.

"How do you know him?" Mary's question became an accusation.

Miriam didn't know why the desire to lie to her friend was so strong. She hadn't done anything wrong.

"That's Michael," she tried to sound as casual as possible. "Don't you know him? He's just a farmhand. He used to be a shepherd boy. I see him sometimes on my walks."

"You know you really shouldn't associate with such people, Miriam ..."

"Oh, I know, but I don't talk to him often. Only if we happen to meet accidently."

"He's also very handsome," Mary had not taken her eyes off him. The distance between them had increased but he still watched them. "Dangerously handsome."

"He's alright, I guess."

"You should be careful, Miriam. You have your reputation to think of. And you're betrothed, remember?"

"How could I forget?" Miriam retorted. "But really, there's nothing to worry about, Mary. He's just a farmhand. What could I possibly want with him?"

"No need to get snappy. I'm just looking out for you. This isn't the first time I've noticed him watching us on our walks. Just how often does he *accidently* find you when you're out here on your own?"

"Oh, I don't know. Every now and then." Miriam felt indignant. 'What does it matter? There's really nothing to worry about. We've talked a few times, that's all. He lost his parents when he was young, so he understands what it is to lose someone you love."

"Oh great, a lonely shepherd boy and a beautiful betrothed young girl wandering the hills together consoling one another. What could possibly go wrong?"

"He's not a shepherd anymore, he's a farmhand. And besides, you worry too much."

"And you don't worry enough," Mary shot back. "If you feel close enough to him to talk about your mother, then you're too close. You're on dangerous ground."

Miriam sighed. She did not want to admit how deep her feelings for Michael went — not even to herself. She did not want to admit how often he appeared in her dreams, and she definitely did not want to admit how she deliberately sought him out on her walks. That his dark eyes sent shockwaves through her heart was something she could barely acknowledge to herself.

"Miriam?" Concern softened Mary's tone.

Miriam nodded, not meeting Mary's gaze. "I guess you're right. I've just been lonely since my mother passed. And Michael has been understanding and kind. But you're right, I know it's foolish. I'm betrothed, whether I like it or not—"

"Just stop for a minute and listen to me." They both stopped walking and stood facing each other in the middle of the dusty trail. Mary placed her hands upon her friend's shoulders, looked into her dark eyes and spoke. "Miriam, I don't think anyone has ever really told you this before, but you are a very beautiful woman – both inside and out. You've inherited your mother's beauty. And with great beauty comes, well, greater responsibility. I see the way the men look at you when we walk past."

A noise of protest escaped Miriam's lips but Mary continued. "Oh, don't scoff, it's true. Even the rabbis gawk at you when they think no one is looking. You must be careful who you bestow your favour on. Men need little encouragement to fall for a beautiful woman. By spending time with him, you're giving him false hope. You know that match can never be. If you care about that shepherd … farmhand … whatever he is – don't encourage him. It can only end badly for both of you."

Miriam stood in shocked silence. She did not think of herself as beautiful, and the way Mary put it made her sound like a temptress, luring poor Michael – oh and the rabbis too – into sin. The thought was horrifying.

"But Michael isn't like other men."

"Really!" It wasn't a question.

"Yes, really. He doesn't see me that way."

"Oh, come on Miriam. He watches you all the time."

"But he calls me his little sister."

"Convenient."

"Fine." Miriam decided to concede defeat. This was going nowhere. Mary would never understand.

"Fine what?" As always, Mary pressed the issue.

"Fine, you're right. I should not have talked to him. It can't end well."

"Okay, what you've done can't be changed. Just be thankful your father hasn't noticed this yet. You must be more careful."

"Alright, I'll not talk to him anymore."

"I'm glad, Miriam. You know I love you, and I only want the best for you." Mary let go of Miriam's shoulders, looped her arm through her friend's, and they continued their progress along the trail.

"I love you too Mary. We should have been sisters." Miriam silently willed herself not to look back to see if Michael was still watching them.

Late that evening, Miriam tiptoed past her father, who was snoring soundly on his sleeping mat. Moving silently, she crept through the courtyard and out the front door.

The moon was high. The town was quiet. Only a few watchmen were on duty. She slipped from house to house, sticking to the shadows, until she reached the trails that led to the farmlands surrounding the town. She began to run towards Michael's uncle's farm. In the silvery light, she could see the familiar paths quite clearly.

She was not much given to moonlight wandering, but this could not wait until morning. She had tried to put her thoughts to rest – tried to sleep. But the conversation with Mary kept her tossing and turning on her sleeping mat.

As her mind churned, Miriam became increasingly convinced that her friend was right. She couldn't pretend anymore. She had been playing with fire, and deep down, she knew it. Perhaps Michael knew it too. But... she didn't want to simply disappear from Michael's life. She wanted to talk to him one last time – if only to put things right between them. She decided to do it straight away, before her resolve weakened. So, she ran on.

Her breath steamed in the cool night air as she crept up to the outbuilding where Michael slept. Despite having moved on from shepherding to heavier work in the fields, Michael had told her he preferred to spend his nights in his old spot in the barn with the sheep.

As Miriam approached, the sheep grew restless. She could hear a few baas from behind the wooden walls of the building. Then Michael peered around the door on high alert as always, a startled expression on his face. His features relaxed when he saw her.

"Miriam?"

"Yes, Michael. It's me."

"What are you doing here?" She could hear the many unspoken questions in his voice.

"I'm sorry. I didn't mean to disturb you. I …" Miriam's words dried up. Her tongue felt thick, and it stuck to the top of her mouth. He emerged from the barn, closing the door silently behind him. He was so close … Moonlight glinted off the black curls that brushed his broad shoulders. His expression was obscured by shadow, but she felt the intensity of his gaze. When he spoke, he sounded annoyed.

"It's the middle of the night. You really shouldn't be here." His words, though true, cut like a knife. She felt like a silly little girl. Miriam took a step back. This wasn't going the way she had planned.

Seeing her fright, Michael softened his voice, "What is it? Is something wrong?" He took a step closer.

"I–I'm sorry. It's nothing. Nothing's wrong. I just…" A lump closed her throat.

In the silence, she sensed Michael weighing up the situation. He gently took hold of her hand, leading her to the rock wall beside the barn. They sat side by side on the wall in the moonlight. Miriam snatched a glance at his face. There was no anger there, only concern. She felt a warm flood of relief.

"Do you know how dangerous this is? Do you know what the punishment would be if we were caught out here together in the middle of the night?"

"I know, but I had to see you." In hushed tones, her eyes gazing fastidiously into her cupped hands, she told him all about her conversation with Mary.

"I have been lonely, Michael. And I've always enjoyed talking to you. I feel safe with you somehow. You're very different from my—" she was going to say father, but she stopped herself. That would be disloyal. "From any other man I've met."

"I thought we were just friends, but today Mary made me realise that what I took for friendship between us has been growing into … well, into something more."

"Miriam—"

"No please, let me finish. I came to tell you I'm betrothed. So, we can't keep meeting any more. We can't talk anymore."

Michael let go of her hand. "But Miriam, of course I know you're betrothed. Besides, even if you weren't, there's no future for us. I'm just a farmhand, and you're the daughter of a scribe."

"Oh, I know that. It's just I have these feelings." There was a heavy silence.

Michael sighed. "I have them too. Do you remember that day we met by the waterfall, all those years ago?" She nodded. "I knew then. Something changed for me that day. I have tried to stay out of your way, but you keep coming into the hills."

"I feel happy when I'm with you."

"Me too, but don't you see it's an impossible dream?"

She stayed silent. She felt humiliated now and wished she hadn't come.

"I have to go." She jumped up. "I'm so sorry. I shouldn't have come. I just wanted to end things on good terms. I won't come looking for you anymore. Goodbye Michael."

He stood up beside her, close enough to touch, looking down at her under the moonlight. He gently tucked a stray curl back beneath her head scarf.

"Goodbye, Miriam," he said, but he did not move away. Instead, he wrapped her up in his arms and drew her to him. The smell of him filled her nostrils. He smelled of wool and dust and sheep, and something uniquely Michael. It was intoxicating. Her face buried into his chest and she drew the scent deep into her lungs.

Miriam felt his hands moving up along her spine; his gentle fingers reaching up beneath her scarf into the curls at the base of her neck. Shivers covered her body as she responded to his touch. They were so close, she could feel his heart beating through his tunic – loud and rapid, like it wanted to burst out of its hiding place.

They stood for a long moment without moving, without breathing. Then she let go, and still facing him, she began her reluctant retreat. There was nothing left to say. No words could fill the gaping hole in her heart. Finally, when she could take it no more, she turned and fled down the road.

When she got to the crossroads, she looked back, silent tears streaming down her cheeks. Michael still stood beside the rock wall – a silver sculpture cast in moonlight. His beauty took her breath away.

She knew that as hard as it was to walk away from him now, living without his presence in her life would be far harder still. Summoning all her will, she kept her eyes on the trail and hurried home.

She tiptoed through the front door of her house thinking she'd made it back safely, then she stifled a scream when she saw her father sitting upright on his sleeping mat. His eyes were ablaze with deep fury.

In that moment, Miriam felt her whole world slipping through her grasp. She had battled her father for control over her life, and now in an instant she knew the battle was over. She had no justifications left that would be any use to her now. No reasons could be given to explain why she was walking back through the front door after midnight. She had just handed her father the trump card. Everything was about to change.

Chapter VI

Light Comes Softly

*When a man wanted to marry a woman in ancient Israel,
Samaritan tradition dictated that he prepare a contract or
covenant to present to the woman and
her father at the their home.*

And then the light comes softly
Dancing through the rain.
It penetrates the grey
To leave the landscape changed.
It exists together with the sorrow
And lives together with the pain.
The light reflects the beauty
As if the balance should remain.
The tension between longing
And the known reality.
The hope and the despair
That are intertwined in all you see.
They dance like faith and unbelief
Illuminating shadows in the grey.
The light thrown to every corner
Where darkness cannot stay.
When understanding of the wrestle
And the tension between lost and found,
The reconstruction of pure joy
Is the sweet gift of accepting
Imperfection's crown.

Miriam – age 19

Miriam had little fight left in her after that night. She had said goodbye to Michael and knew it was final, so when her father insisted that she hasten the wedding plans, Miriam had no choice but to agree. The necessary arrangements were quickly put in place.

Within two short months, the wedding ceremony commenced. The scene was chaotic. Miriam stood at the centre of an elaborately decorated room as people swirled all around her like bees around the queen at the centre of the hive.

Women came, shook her hands and touched her cheeks, singing and praying aloud before drifting back into the crowd. Miriam endured it all silently. Though surrounded by friends and family members, she felt like a stranger watching the proceedings from a distance.

Now that she stood in attendance at her own wedding ceremony, she felt as if she was being drawn towards the edge of a precipice, all too aware that she was about to fall over the edge. Ahead lay nothing but uncertainty.

Her life had slipped from her hands and into the hands of the man who stood beside her. His intentions unclear. His heart an unknown entity. His nature, be it kind or cruel, would dictate her fate. She yearned for her mother. She longed to be out in the wild – to run into the desert and never come home. At least nature had a certain predictability.

Despite being showered with prayers and well wishes, Miriam struggled to suppress the tears that threatened to fall. When her father had covered her face with the veil just prior to the ceremony, she felt relieved.

Hidden behind the soft folds of material, she felt a little safer, though with each passing minute her fear and anxiety threatened to choke her. Every invisible tear, though veiled from sight, fell down into the canyon of her heart.

While the priest droned on about the significance of marriage, Miriam glanced sideways at the man who was about to become her husband and, if all went according to tradition, would be the father of her many children. Caleb's face was set in a serious expression. He was an attractive man, tall and strong, but she could not tell what he might be thinking. There was no visible emotion on the canvas of his skin. No give away glint in his eyes. He stood looking at the priest as if he was lining himself up to swat a fly that had landed on the man's head.

Caleb was from a village on the other side of the Jordan River. At their betrothal ceremony several months earlier, he had offered her the betrothal cup. In accordance with tradition, she took it from his hands and held it to her lips. Thus, they were betrothed. At the time, the room had erupted in applause as friends and family celebrated their now unbreakable bond.

Unbidden, images of Michael came into her mind. Michael sitting beside her on the flat rock. Michael hugging the cliff next to the waterfall. Michael with his adoring sheep. Michael bathed in moonlight beside the barn's rock wall the last time she saw him. She shook her head in disbelief at how naïve she had been, refusing to accept that it was her duty to get married. Thinking she could avoid this day. Fighting against the inevitable and instead allowing her heart to be swept away in fantasy. All her arguments and delay tactics had been in vain.

Now, she finally understood the strength of the currents of tradition and duty that carried all their lives onward towards their destinies. As Miriam stood in her own wedding ceremony looking at Caleb, she felt like a twig carried by a mighty river ever onward to the sea.

Later that evening, when the madness of the ceremony was over, a terrified Miriam entered their bed chamber. She didn't know what to expect, but Caleb surprised her. He smiled and invited her to sit down next to him.

"How are you feeling?" he asked gently.

"Um, I …" Miriam shrugged and stared at her hands.

"It's okay, Miriam. You can speak freely to me." He wrapped her small hands in his large ones. "I want you to know how happy I am that you are my wife. I only pray that in time you will also be happy. Now, tell me truthfully, are you tired?" His reassuring words and gentle tone broke through her defences.

"A little, I guess."

"Me too." She remained silent and stared intently down at their intwined hands as he continued. "You know, from the moment I first saw you, I knew you were special. You are a beautiful woman, and I want to be a good husband to you, Miriam."

She looked up at him, tears brimming in her eyes. Caleb squeezed her hands gently.

"I was so sorry to hear about your mother's passing."

"Thank you." Miriam nodded, and two large tears splashed down onto his wrist.

"I know you've been unhappy about marrying me, and I'm sorry," he added after a pause. "I never wanted to force you onto this."

"My father did." The bitter comment slipped out before she could bite it back. Caleb let it pass.

"I promise you, our marriage will be a blessing to you. My heart is overjoyed by the prospect of having you in my life, and I intend to do everything in my power to ensure that you will share my joy. You see, I plan to win you over with love and respect – not just in public, but also behind closed doors."

Miriam was slightly stunned by how diplomatically he had let her know that he understood her fears. She wasn't quite sure whether she could believe his promise to love and respect her, but the words did sound sweet.

As though reading her thoughts, Caleb added, "I

know they are just words to you right now, and it may be hard for you to believe me, but I am sincere. I don't expect you to trust me right away. It will take time, I know. In the meantime, know this: I will never intentionally hurt you."

She looked deep into Caleb's dark eyes and knew instinctively that he was sincere. In the presence of this handsome man, so at ease in himself, Miriam began to feel herself relax.

"Thank you. I do want to be a good wife to you," she said and was surprised to find that she really meant it.

His smile made his face even more handsome. He raised her hands to his lips and planted gentle kisses on her fingers. Miriam looked into his eyes once more.

"We can be happy, Miriam. We can have a good life together, and as we get to know each other, we will come to love one another, I'm sure of it. I know it's hard to see now, but in time, we will have children and build a home and a legacy … together."

Miriam could feel the heat moving up her cheeks as his lips caressed her fingers. Caleb pulled her closer into an embrace and held her gently, his breath landing warm on her neck. "Is this, okay?" he asked as he began to kiss her neck. Miriam was surprised at the warm feeling that rose within her at his touch and she did not pull away.

She knew a little of what was expected of her on her wedding night, but he led the way with a gentleness she had never known possible in a man. Her mind turned over and over, but she closed her eyes and let him guide her.

Chapter VII

Always A Goodbye

Psalm 46 (NIV)
[1] *God is our refuge and strength,*
an ever-present help in trouble.
[2] *Therefore we will not fear, though the earth give way*
and the mountains fall into the heart of the sea,
[3] *though its waters roar and foam*
and the mountains quake with their surging.
[4] *There is a river whose streams make glad the city of God,*
the holy place where the Most High dwells.
[5] *God is within her, she will not fall;*
God will help her at break of day.
[6] *Nations are in uproar, kingdoms fall;*
he lifts his voice, the earth melts.
[7] *The Lord Almighty is with us;*
the God of Jacob is our fortress.
[8] *Come and see what the Lord has done,*
the desolations he has brought on the earth.
[9] *He makes wars cease*
to the ends of the earth.
He breaks the bow and shatters the spear;
he burns the shields with fire.

¹⁰ He says, "Be still, and know that I am God;
I will be exalted among the nations,
I will be exalted in the earth."
¹¹ The Lord Almighty is with us;
the God of Jacob is our fortress.

There is always a goodbye
Waiting at the end
Of every single person
You have known as friend.

There is always a full stop
At every finish line,
Where you must start again
And leave the past behind.

And though some friends will walk beside you
Further down the road,
It is a solo journey
On which the soul must go.

So, for every sweet hello
There will be a last goodbye.
Every door will close
While you are still alive.

But for every bitter end,
There is the start of something new.
As daylight follows night
So an end proceeds a breakthrough.

As every seed gives up its life
To let the new glimpse light of day,
So every end must be complete
Before the new comes by your way.

And while we wrestle with each loss
It's in the letting go that we discover,
The soul is most content
When poured out freely for each other.

To give away
To gift
To choose sacrifice
And leak our care,
Is the most courageous
Choice to make
When life will not play fair.

To pre-empt every loss
By giving love away
Is the bravest way a heart can live
As it journeys onwards
Through each day.

Miriam – age 21

In the two years since their marriage, Miriam had settled into life with Caleb in a way that she had never imagined possible. It seemed that even her need for wild places had been tamed. She no longer yearned to go wandering around in the hills and gladly carried out her domestic duties. The comfort, consistency, and peace of her new home, away from her father, was an unexpected gift.

She loved spending time with Mary and the other women on their daily walks to the well, and though she was still as close as ever to Mary, Caleb had become her dearest friend. She had allowed her heart to love him. Everyday she looked forward to sunset when he would come home. She would curl up beside him like a child, and he would tell her stories of his life as a soldier – his travels through Samaria and Judah. How exciting his life was!

She missed him when he was away with his regiment. During his absence, she would sleep with her arms wrapped around one of his tunics, so she could smell his scent and imagine he was there beside her.

"How quickly the heart can change. How quickly life can change. How fast seasons come and go." Miriam spoke the words into a hot August wind as she hung out her sheets to dry.

She was in the common area not far from her home, not far from where the trails began into the hills. She looked up towards the flat rock and for a moment thought that she saw someone standing there looking down at her. In the bright sunlight she blinked and rubbed her eyes, trying to clear them of the desert's gritty dryness. When she looked up again, no one was there.

"Mirage," she muttered under her breath, but she couldn't deny that her mind flashed almost instinctively towards Michael. She wondered where he was and what had kept him occupied since she had last seen him. *Was he still working at his uncle's farm? Had he left Sychar? Did he know she was married? Did he care?*

She shook her head and tried to gather up her scattered thoughts like the folds of her washing. "I am married to Caleb. He is such a good man. Such a kind husband." Thoughts of Michael soon disappeared as she remembered the many reasons she was thankful for Caleb.

Her mother had been right all along. If only she had listened and agreed to the marriage earlier. It would have made her mother so happy to see her settled and in a home of her own. She'd had the power to release her mother from worry and she had fought and resisted it like a spoilt child.

Miriam had not realised that her mother could see much further down the road than her young mind had been capable of. She had stubbornly refused to listen or trust her, thinking she knew better – or perhaps not really thinking at all. Her fears had ruled her and driven her away from any reasoning her mother attempted to offer. Miriam sighed. She wished things had been different for her mother in the end.

Her grief had transformed itself into a heavy burden of regrets. They hung around her shoulders, invisible, but there nonetheless. She knew there was no point dragging them around with her, but she couldn't release herself from their guilt-ridden grip.

She clipped the last sheet up over the rope rigging and felt the material flutter against her arms and face. The intensity of summer was slowly beginning to ebb away, but as the wind blew in gusts like a warm breath over the sands, she knew the sheets would be dry in no time. Miriam picked up the empty washing basket and headed back to town. Suddenly she stopped in surprise when she saw a familiar face standing a short distance away.

"Oh." Miriam gaped.

"Miriam," her father's face was drawn and serious. She sucked in her breath. "Mary told me you might be here."

Miriam nodded, taken aback by his uncharacteristic appearance. She had not seen him in months, and her stomach turned over with a strange and uneasy feeling that something was terribly wrong. She waited for him to explain.

"I am sorry Miriam, but there is bad news," he stepped forward.

Miriam felt her heart start racing inside her chest. "What is it?" A lump stuck in her throat preventing any further sound from coming out.

He continued slowly. "It's Caleb. He has been injured in an accident. You must come quickly."

Speechless, she stared in horror at her father and dropped the empty washing basket. He moved forward and took her elbow and she was surprised by the gentleness of his touch as he led her on towards the town.

"Come, he is asking for you. There is very little time."

Miriam's heart galloped in her chest. *Very little time?* She had no clear thoughts, only an overarching feeling of panic, and a terrible need to escape. She felt like running as fast and as far as she could into the hills. Anything to escape the pain that threatened to overcome her.

With great difficulty, she subdued the urge and allowed her father to lead her. Her legs felt like liquid under her body and if it had not been for his hands holding her arm, she would have surely fallen.

They reached a small house on the outskirts of town. Moving inside, she found Caleb laying on a sleeping mat. She knelt beside him and took one of his hands in hers.

"Caleb?" She touched his forehead with her fingertips and stroked his hair as though he were a child and she, his mother.

"Miriam?" Caleb's voice was weak. His eyes found hers. He tried to smile but instead tears welled up and spilled over his cheeks.

"I'm here." Miriam's face was wet with her own tears. She knuckled them away then returned to stroking his hair.

"I love you, Miriam. I'm so sorry …"

"No, Caleb. No, no. Please, don't leave me."

Caleb closed his eyes. His grip on her hand loosened. One final exhale and he let go completely. Silently, she begged him to take another breath, but he did not. The light of his spirit had been extinguished. Miriam searched for it in his face, his eyes, his lips. But he was gone.

The shock and finality of it all stung Miriam to the core. She hung her head and sobbed, feeling like she had been punched in the chest. "No, no, no, no, no," she repeated over and over as her mind wrestled with this new reality. Suddenly, an image of the sheets fluttering out in the hot August wind of the desert flashed into her mind. The winds of change were blowing.

She had tried so hard to be a good wife, to love Caleb, and to make their marriage a happy one. She had given him everything she had to give. And yet, it had all been taken from her. Once again, the person she loved most in the world was gone, and she was left with empty hands and an aching heart. Was she never to escape this prison of grief? Miriam felt detached from reality, terrified and desperately alone. In her mind, she was falling into a bottomless void – a canyon so deep she could no longer see the light.

"Miriam." Her father's a hand on her shoulder made her jump.

"Leave me."

"Miriam, you need to come away now."

She put her arms around her dead husband, pressed her cheek into his chest and sobbed. Her father tried to pull her away, but she clung to her beloved.

"Miriam?" Her father's voice had a glint of its former metal in it now. It struck a chord in her soul and instinct took over. She let go of Caleb and allowed her father to raise her to her feet. Leaning heavily on him, she let herself be ushered out of the room.

She looked back at her husband one final time and only then noticed that there were others in the room. Soldiers. They stood with eyes downcast. Someone had closed his eyes and from the other side of the room he appeared to be sleeping peacefully. For an instant her heart leapt. Perhaps that was it? Perhaps he was not really dead, only sleeping? She turned, ready to run back to him, but her father's arm tightened around her, and the door closed behind them.

Her husband was gone. She was in shock that felt like it paralised her whole being. A widow. All alone in this desolate place. His sudden departure enveloped her like a suffocating fog.

Chapter VIII

Moments

Joshua 1:9
"Have I not commanded you? Be strong and courageous. Do not be afraid; do not be discouraged, for the LORD your God will be with you wherever you go."

It's the tiny moments we pivot on
That quietly define our lives.
The weight of the insignificant
Hidden deep in plain disguise.
It's the dreams that fall
Right through the cracks
While we're trying to hold on.
The thing we can't get back
As time marches us along.
The unimportant decisions
Determine who we will become.
The little things we overlook
Add up to an insurmountable sum.
And we pivot
And we turn
And we dance
Down the trail,
That will lead us step by step
Over the mountains we travail.
We choose our own restrains
As the seasons move us on,
And store the broken remnants
To remind us what we got so wrong.
We make the best and then look back
In hindsight just to see
That we might have missed
The joy of it,
Too busy gazing out to sea.

A shift in time
A breath.
A word that leaves us cold.
The ones who walk away
And the ones we watch grow old.
The child who once
Wore your skin
With eyes now getting old,
Can still feel the anticipation
Of time waiting to unfold.
It's the delusion
Of the moment
That makes us miss
What is right here,
As we fuss and hold in balance
All of our love and fear.
So let us take a step
Deliberately and slow.
As we pivot on the choices
Of this single narrow road.

Miriam – age 21

Miriam stood at Caleb's grave, her hands clasped in front of her; her eyes downcast. In the six weeks since his passing, an aching numbness had come over her.

Each time the rawness of the grief threatened to overwhelm, her heart locked away the pain. She was afraid of grief and did not want to feel the deep sorrow she had felt when her mother died. Ever again! It was instinctual. It was survival. She had retreated into numbness. At first it had been a welcome companion, but now, at times, it caused an aching well to open up within her soul that longed to be filled.

Endless and unanswerable questions asailed her without mercy. She wondered why God had given her a loving husband only to take him away so soon. What was the point? Was God tormenting her for a reason? Was this punishment for her sins? In the face of such questions without answers, a sense of hopeless resignation engulfed her.

She felt utterly adrift. Stuck in an emotional limbo in a world that no longer made any sense to her. The control she'd delusionally believed that she had over her own destiny, was slipping away from her bit by bit. She was back under her father's dominion, and yet, she no longer seemed to care. It all seemed so futile. She was bone weary. Too tired to fight.

Now, as she stood once again with her beloved

husband's grave before her, she willed herself to feel something. Anything.

"I miss you so much. I wish you were here. How can you be gone? I don't know what to do without you."

Some tiny part of her listened to the soft breeze as if almost expecting him to answer. She sighed and crumpled to her knees.

"Oh, why did you leave me?" Miriam was surprised at the anger she suddenly felt rise within her. "How could you be so selfish." She wailed. Her fists balled by her sides; her nails dug into the soft flesh of her palms. Just as swiftly as it had come, the anger subsided to be replaced by immense sorrow and remorse.

"I'm sorry," she gulped. "It's just that I'm so lonely without you. Oh, my love, I only want to feel your arms around me once more. To hear you tell me that it will all be okay." A single tear ran slowly down Miriam's cheek, and with it, her resistance crumbled. She finally gave in to the pain, anger and sorrow of her grief.

Memories of their time together pierced her consciousness like lightning strikes through storm clouds. She mourned them all. Images of the future they could have had together came to haunt her, and she wept for that too. She let herself cry and rage for all of it. She cried until her eyes were red raw and puffy, and she had no tears left.

The sunrise glinted low and orange across the sands. She rubbed her hands over her swollen face and stood up. To the east, the sun lifted its skirts free from the horizon casting red orange hews across the desert floor.

Miriam knew she should go home to prepare breakfast for her father, but instead, she turned towards the foothills. She had not wandered up onto the trails for several years, and yet, she knew the paths as though they were lines on the face of an old friend. As she walked, she felt the hills welcome her in their undemanding, unconditional embrace. Here she could be free of her father's constant badgering, the pity of her friends and relatives, and most of all, the town gossip.

She despised the sad staring townsfolk with their feigned sorrow that served only as an excuse to whisper about her.

"Such a shame. Him such a good man."

"Oh, yes. And her childless. What's to be done now?"

"Perhaps a second wife to one of Caleb's brothers?"

"He has none."

"Oh dear."

"Can't expect that father of hers will keep her much longer. He'll find someone to take her off his hands."

Although they would say it all behind her back, they had nothing to say to her at all. Instead, they turned away from her, keeping their eyes on the ground, pretending they did not see her.

Being alone in the trails in the wilderness felt like a homecoming for her soul.

As she walked, Miriam began to breathe deeply.

It felt good to be moving. She had missed the physical exertion of hill walking and was surprised by how out of breath she quickly became. She hadn't even reached the flat rock before her legs begged for rest, but she ignored their protests.

Once at the rock, she stopped and took a moment to look back on the town. She could see people beginning to emerge from their homes and the steady trickle of women walking towards the well. She could see the house she and Caleb had lived in, and the area towards the base of the rocks where she had been hanging her sheets on the day her father came to find her. She could see her father's house a short distance away and guessed that he would soon be waking and angry that she was not there, ready and waiting with water from the well and the morning meal prepared for him. She didn't care.

Turning away from the town, she followed the trail to the little oasis that had been her favourite childhood haunt. On the other side of the oasis, the trail led through a patch of scraggly bush before winding its way down the hillside into a wide valley below.

Miriam zigzagged her way down the steep trail, glancing up every now and then to take in the view. She spotted the barn where Michael used to sleep. Had she really run all that way in the middle of the night? She had been so young and foolish back then. A silly infatuated girl. She wondered idly whether he might be around, then pushed that idea firmly from her mind. She did not even want to think about Michael, let alone see him. She had come here to get away from everyone, Michael included.

The valley was mysterious, long and beautiful – a dark green line on the desert's golden face, it gracefully curved around the foothills until it vanished into the distant horizon.

Feeling lighter with every step, she found and followed the river as it made its lazy way along the bottom of the valley. Although she was aware that she had gone further than ever before, still her feet kept moving. Walking quelled her troubled thoughts and stilled her soul. What did it matter where she was going or what she would find? No one back home would miss her. In fact, they would likely be relieved to be rid of her.

Every so often she paused to drink from little eddies in the river. The water was surprisingly cool and refreshing. She wanted to stop and take in the rhythm of the river's movements, but something inside willed her on. She pushed forward for several hours, until the sun was warm overhead, and her sandaled feet begged for rest.

At midday, she rounded a bend and came upon a cluster of poplar trees whose branches had twined overhead to form a leafy canopy over a shady glade. Their leaves danced and glinted like sparkling emeralds, while roots, like long fingers, dipped down the crumbling riverbank into the cool water below.

Miriam let out a long sigh of wonder and delight at the beauty before her. Feeling as though she were walking into someone's home without knocking, she gingerly picked her way through the thicket between the tree trunks and stepped into the glade.

A huge tree stood in the centre, its broad-leafed branches stretched skyward in an attitude of praise before stretching out to entwine with the other tree branches. Miriam walked up to the tree and ran her fingers across its rough green bark.

With the green canopy above her and soft grass beneath her feet, she realised she had found the sanctuary she'd been searching for all day. "Heaven." Her heart filled with bittersweet gratitude at the discovery of this leafy hideaway beneath the age-old trees.

She stretched out on the grass, giving her aching limbs a much-needed rest. She glimpsed snatches of blue sky between the thick foliage and dappled sunlight played upon her eyelids as they gradually closed.

Half hidden in the long grass, Miriam curled up on her side, wrapped her arms around herself, and imagined that she lay in a place no one else could reach; where she could stay forever in peace and blend into the earth itself. Waves of exhaustion washed over her, and she slipped gently into sleep. The only sound, that of the trickling river as it journeyed endlessly toward some distant sea.

Miriam jerked awake. Had she heard something? A rustling? She held her breath and lay ridged beneath the canopy of tree branches. She strained her ears and heard the unmistakable sound of human footsteps coming towards her hiding place. They stopped just outside the circle of trees. Daylight had faded while she slept, and she could just make out the shape of a man beside one of the tree trunks.

She almost cried out, "Who's there?" But clamped a hand over her mouth before she could give herself away. She had been warned about the thieves and outcasts who lived in the wilds beyond the town, and the violent things they would do to a girl out on her own. Miriam had blithely ignored these warnings. Would she now pay the price for her folly?

The thought of a potential attack forced her to her feet. Pressing her back against the trunk of the tree, not taking her eyes off the shadow for a moment, she grappled for the knife she kept in her leather satchel. It was not very large, but sharp as mustard and big enough to deliver a nasty cut to anyone who came within arm's reach. She stood poised with the knife, ready to strike as soon as the intruder made his move. She hoped desperately that he would go away and leave her alone, but to her horror, he scrambled through the undergrowth towards her. She gave a high piercing cry and ran at him, swinging the blade in a wide downward arc. He raised a hand in defence. The blade slashed through the skin of his forearm. The man cried out in pain and grasped his bleeding arm. Their eyes met, and Miriam gasped.

"Michael." Her mouth formed a perfect "o".

"Miriam." He grimaced. Still clutching his arm. Drops of blood sparkled like rubies in the grass.

"You cut me." He looked at the knife in her hand, incredulous.

"Well, you startled me." Miriam's fear gave way to sudden anger that rose like heat off the desert floor. They both stood motionless, panting, staring in horror at Michael's bleeding forearm. Remorse overtook her anger, and she dropped the knife. She went over to him.

"I'm sorry. Let me see it." He proffered his injured limb. She took it gently in her own, staring down at the red river of blood that coursed down his wrist. She turned her gaze back up at him, concern etched across her features.

"It's nothing," he assured her. "Just a superficial cut. I'll be alright." Taking his arm back, he went over to the river and washed the blood away before wrapping the wound in the strip of cloth torn from his tunic. It wasn't nothing, but she said no more.

"What are you doing here?" he asked over his shoulder.

"I could ask you the same," she shot back.

"I followed you," he answered as he scrambled back up the bank and came towards her, pinning her with his frank, unapologetic gaze.

"You followed me?"

"Yes." He did not smile, instead he looked grave.

"You shouldn't have." She tossed her head and folded her arms across her chest.

"I was worried about you."

"Well, I'm perfectly fine. So, you can go now. I know my way back."

"Perfectly fine and fast asleep," came the barbed reply. "Just what would you have done if I had been a bandit? Cut me to pieces with that puny knife of yours?"

"I can defend myself!" His criticism chafed at her pride.

"Stop acting like a spoiled child. You know, you are the most infuriating …" He closed his eyes and pinched his nose between the thumb and forefinger. "Oh, just forget it." He shook his head, turned his back on her and started walking away. Then he stopped and turned to face her once more.

"You should probably know that I wasn't the only one following you today."

"Really?" The word was laced with sarcasm.

"Yes, really. A mountain lion was on your trail too. I killed it, but there are others sculking around. You may not be as lucky next time. Just thought you should know." He took several more steps away, then turned again. "Oh, and by the way, you've also wandered all this way without giving a thought to how long it will take you to get back. It will be dark before you reach the village."

"Thanks for your concern, but I can look

after myself," Miriam huffed. She knew she was being unreasonable, but she didn't care. He'd annoyed her by pointing out that she was not as wise to the ways of nature as she thought.

Michael came towards her. "No," he said simply. "No, you can't." His voice was calmer now. "You're vulnerable out here on your own. And I plan to make sure you get back home safely – whether you like it or not."

"Home? I don't have a home anymore." She hung her head.

"I know you've been through a lot." He took another step towards her.

Now he was so close they were almost touching. His physicality made it hard for her to think straight. Her heart pounded like a wild horse in her chest. What was it about him that unsettled her so?

"You know, you truly are a beautiful young woman," he suddenly said, gently pushing a wilful curl back beneath her headscarf. "Far too beautiful for an old farmhand like me."

"You're not that old," she scoffed.

"I feel old. A thousand years old. And you're not a little girl anymore." He took her hand in his. Miriam knew she should pull away, but instead she let him lift her hand and press his palm to hers. They stood palm-to-palm, transfixed in the darkening space beneath the trees for a long time.

She felt the strange energy between them increase

and reverberate through her body. She tried to break free from his gaze, tried to snatch her hand away, but she could not move.

Eventually, he broke the spell. Without a word, he dropped his hand and moved away, leaving her standing with her hand raised as though in farewell. Then his features changed, his face brightened, and the moment had passed. She lowered her hand.

"Come, little sis. Let's get you home." Though his voice sounded gruff, he had used the old pet name he'd given her all those years ago. He gestured for her to go ahead of him. "I'll follow you to the edge of town. You should be safe from there. I'll stay a good distance away so no one sees me, but close enough to spot another mountain lion."

Her face burning with a strange mixture of shame and longing, she silently led the way. Miriam did not need to turn around, she knew that he would be there, right behind her.

Chapter IX

You Are Not Hidden

Leviticus 20:10-12 (NIV)

If a man commits adultery with another man's wife — with the wife of his neighbour — both the adulterer and adulteress are to be put to death.

You are not hidden,
though you may try desperately to hide.
You are not useless,
though you may not realise the worth
that you carry inside.
You are not pointless,
though you may debate what
the point is each day.
You are not hopeless,
though the hope you once held,
appears to have run far away.

In fact, you are seen
You are held
You are known.
Your life is a gift
Like a seed
That is sown.
You are precious and loved
Far beyond what you believe.
You are valued
Beyond measure.
You have your own destiny.

Miriam – age 25

Pain registered in her heart before she felt the sting of it across her cheek. Miriam instinctively put her hands up to her face and leant away, shocked and terrified by the coldness in his eyes.

Nirgal stood over her, an expression of disgust on his face. Miriam crouched, her hands raise in defence against another blow. It never came. It took her a moment to realise he had backed off and was pacing back and forth like a caged lion, muttering as he did so.

"Why do I put up with you? You are a useless wife. Useless. What do I profit from this marriage? Where are my sons? Where are my heirs? Four years and I do not even have a lousy daughter from you. I have been patient with you, have I not? I could have divorced you and moved on years ago, but ah the shame … And I have my family's reputation to think of – do I not? Besides …" He grasped her chin in his large hand and turned her head this way and that. "Your beauty makes a fool out of me." He let her go so roughly that she fell sideways onto the earth floor. "My friends told me to find myself another woman, but I chose to wait and see. I've grown tired of waiting," he growled. "I'm sick and tired of you."

She had just made it back onto her knees when a fresh blow struck the edge of her jaw. This time, she saw stars twinkling as the darkness engulfed her.

Miriam came around some time later, lying on the cold hard floor. A jagged shard of shame stabbed her to the core. The pain was as familiar to her as the physical cuts and bruises dealt from his hands, but she felt the shame far more often and more keenly than any physical pain he had ever delivered to her. It pierced her heart when she walked with Mary and her two little children to the well. It twisted like a knife in her gut when she saw young mothers at the marketplace with babies wrapped tightly on their backs, arms full of vegetables and a line of other children in tow, like ducklings following a mother duck. And she felt it might rip her apart when confronted by the undisguised disappointment in her father's face.

Naïvely, she'd spent four years hoping things might change, that she might fall pregnant, or at least, be forgiven for being barren. But the only thing that had changed was her husband's increasingly hostile and aggressive behaviour towards her and her growing conviction that she was an utter failure as a wife.

Miriam didn't know what was wrong with her. Perhaps this barren state was her punishment? Afterall, she had been a sinful woman – a fornicator who deserved to be stoned.

That encounter with Michael in the glade had been but the first of many. She had been drawn back there shortly after that day, and to her surprise, Michael had been waiting for her. At first, their trysts had been innocent enough, but they had rapidly become more intimate. Eventually, they had let their passions run free. She had lain with him as with a husband. Not just once, although she constantly promised herself and God that each time would be the last. Still, she had returned to the glade and each time, he had found her there.

Of course, it had all come to an end when her father arranged for her to be married to Nirgal. Like her father, Nirgal was an upstanding member of the Samaritan community and a devout follower of their religious principles. And, like her father, he was a tyrant. Rules and regulations governed every aspect of their life and foremost among them was her obligation to provide him with an heir. As a man of great expectations, though little gentleness, it had not been from the lack of trying that she failed to conceive.

After a year had gone by with no child to show for his efforts, Nirgal had redoubled his trips to the temple, making ever more impressive and expensive sacrifices in hope that God would bless him with a child.

Each time her monthly cycle arrived instead of a child, Miriam would weep and begin a new month of steadfast prayer and fasting, beseeching God to bless them.

Nirgal was wealthy, and came from a family who enjoyed good standing in the community. He was his parents' only surviving son and they desperately wanted him to produce an heir to ensure that their seat on the council would remain with the family.

Finally, Nirgal had concluded that God's apparent refusal to bestow on him an heir, meant that God was displeased by his union with Miriam, and it did not take Nirgal long to blame his wife and let his own eyes go wandering to other prospects.

Now, as she lay before him, a pitiful mess, he despised her more than ever. "It must be because of your mixed blood," he declared. "I should have known it. Naturally, God won't bless our union because you are unclean."

Miriam sucked in her breath sharply, and she had heard her own father say this same thing to her mother so many times before. Her worst fear had come true – she was living her mother's life, trapped in a loveless marriage with a man who hated her and there was nothing she could do about it.

She wanted more than anything to be accepted and loved, and yet his words had laid bare the very crux of the matter: she was inherently impure, shameful, unworthy of love, rejected by God because of her bloodline and she admitted privately, because of her wayward nature.

"I need a true Samaritan wife. One whom God will bless with many children. One who will bring me honour among men."

"Tell me what to do, and I will do it."

"There is nothing you can do. It is your blood. You can't change that. I'll have no more of your pleading and tears. Get out. You are no longer my wife." The finality of these words left Miriam stunned. They meant he had divorced her. All he needed to do now was to make it official by returning her dowry to her father.

Unable to move or speak, she watched as he stormed out of their small house. Then panic overtook her at the thought of what her father might do to her when he heard of the divorce. She would bring disgrace upon him, and he would hate her even more. She rushed after Nirgal. Shouting his name, she followed him outside, but Nirgal was not about to be humiliated in public.

He stopped and turned around, a thunderous look on his face, then stormed over to her as she retreated into the house once more. He entered and closed the door behind him. Miriam shrank away from him, but he was faster, and before she knew it, he had her by the shoulders. His fingers dug painfully into her flesh. He pulled her close, and hissed into her ear, "Don't you ever dare embarrass me in public like that again. Haven't I endured enough already? You will be gone before I return. Do you understand?" She whimpered her agreement through shaking lips. He released her, pushing her to the ground, and strode out the door.

For a long time, Miriam stayed where he had thrown her. She brought her knees up to her chest and crossed her arms over them the way she used to do when she was a child. She stared absently at the peeling wall on the far side of the room, noticing that the ugly bits of mud and stone were visible in patches where the whitewash had peeled away. She cried softly at the stark symbolism. By ending the relationship with Michael and getting married to a respected member of the community, she had tried to whitewash her life and cover over all of her sins. But the whitewash had worn thin, and the ugly patches of her past were threatening to break through.

Her body began to shake with a strange mixture of fear and relief – as though she had been holding her breath for a long time and had finally been allowed to let it go. Though she did not know what lay ahead, at least she would be free of Nirgal. That thought left her giddy.

Then she wondered, would he really go through with the divorce? The shame of it would mar his family's social standing. They may try to stop him. But now that she had tasted freedom, she could not go back. She wanted to be rid of him, once and for all.

She knew what she had to do. There was only one way to be free and avoid her father's wrath – she had to leave Sychar. It would be hard, but it would be best for everyone. The divorce need not be made public. Nirgal would be rid of her without losing face. He could take a new wife and get the son he longed for. Perhaps that would make him happy and less prone to aggression? Perhaps nothing would change him. She did not care, she would not be around to find out.

She stood up and grabbed her leather satchel off its hook. It still contained her small knife. Seeing the silvery blade, she recalled the nasty cut on Michael's arm and shuddered involuntarily.

Moving quickly now, she headed to the storeroom and stuffed a few loaves and some fruit into the satchel. Reaching to the very back of the bottom shelf, she felt around beneath a pile of old cleaning cloths until her fingers touched the hard edge of a small package. She tucked it into her satchel and left the house without a backward glance.

Though the uncertain future terrified her, as soon as she stepped out of the front door, Miriam felt a weight lift from her shoulders. She knew she would never return. Could never return. But it no longer mattered to her. In fact, the further she walked from the house, the more she began to wonder why she had stayed. Why had she put up with his cruelty for so long? Why had she waited for him to say those words? And how she wished now that she had found the courage to leave much sooner.

Chapter X

Back To The Beginning

Shechem is a city located in the hill country of Ephraim. The city lies in a fertile valley between the mountains of Gerizim and Ebal. Due to its central location in the middle of the nation, it was a crossroads for travel to various destinations around Israel.

Go back to the beginning
And unravel it like a piece of string.
Work out all the knots
And weave the wandering frays back in.

Don't be afraid to ask the questions
And face the answers as they come.
Though history cannot be changed
Your future has only just begun.

Unpack the darkest hours
That you've buried far too deep.
Let them out into the light
And take the lessons you need to keep.

For even the hardest journeys
Have helped to make you who you are.
So go back to the beginning,
Understand the road that's lead this far.

Then stand at this new crossroads
With your eyes lifted high,
Free from the burdens you have carried
For you've unravelled all the "whys".

How long is a piece of string?
How long is one single life?
Each of your days are numbered
And you can never live one twice.

So let this be the line you draw
With a new vision out in front of you
For the journey isn't over yet
And today could be your breakthrough.

Miriam – age 25

From the old well at one end, to the foothills at the other, Miriam knew every nook and cranny of Sychar's buildings and dusty streets. This place had been her entire world – all of her memories, good and bad, were contained within its walls. She knew every house, the quickest routes around the town, and most of the community. And they knew her.

Although Caleb had told her about far flung places, she had seen them only in her imagination. So, the excitement she felt at the prospect of finally seeing new parts of the country was tainted by a feeling of nostalgia. Although she had railed against them all her life, she now realised how much she would miss the comfort of her familiar surroundings. Still, she walked on.

Suddenly there was a hand on her shoulder. She turned to find Neriah, Sheerah and Mary by her side.

"Miriam," Neriah slipped her arm around Miriam's waist, and they walked side by side down the dusty road. "Are you alright? You walked right past us without a word. You have a nasty bruise on your jaw, and you're white as a sheet. What has happened?"

Miriam choked back the tears that sprang to her eyes in the face of her friends' concern and told them, in as few words as possible, the things that had happened that morning and her decision to leave Nirgal and Sychar for good.

"I'm going to stay with my aunt. It's the only option I have."

"It's good you have your aunt to go to. My mother once knew a woman who ran away from her husband. She had nowhere to go, and she ended up alone and destitute," said Neriah. "They eventually found her body out in the desert. She'd been preyed on by bandits and just left for dead…"

"Neriah, that's not necessary," scolded Mary.

Miriam shuddered at the thought of a woman dying alone and gasping for her last breaths out in the wilderness. She tried to shake the image out of her mind. "Let's keep walking."

Mary squeezed her hand reassuringly. "It's for the best, Miriam. We know how badly he treated you. This is the only way you'll ever be free of him."

"Even my husband is only friendly to his face. Behind closed doors he doesn't have many good things to say about Nirgal," Sheerah whispered as if the trees had ears and then added more emphatically, "You will be okay."

"Yes," said Neriah. "You're very brave."

"You're doing what's best for you," said Mary.

"I wish I knew that."

"Deep down, I think you do," Mary continued. "This town was always too small for you, my adventurous friend. You need freedom and open spaces. You'll find happiness eventually. Just trust in God, He will not let you fall."

"I am already fallen. I've had two marriages and no children. Everyone in Sychar thinks I'm impure. People whisper behind my back. I feel their judgment and their pity, and I don't know which is worse. But what if they are right? What will I do then?"

"In your new town, things will be different. No one will know your history. You are still so beautiful; you will find a good man. Only believe that God will take care of all your needs," said Mary.

"And, your aunt will take care of you too," Sheerah added.

"I think I'm going to be the one taking care of her." Miriam had only met her aunt once before. Her memory of their meeting had been blurred by the passage of time, and she could not recall having any warm feelings towards her mother's older sister.

But knowing that she was elderly and would likely welcome an able-bodied niece to help around the house, Miriam had decided to throw herself on her aunt's mercy. And, since her mother's side of the family had been estranged from her during her marriage to Miriam's father, she thought it was unlikely that the old woman would send messages to her father concerning her whereabouts.

"She is crippled and needs help. So, I think she'll let me work for my board and lodging. Besides, without my dowry, I really can't get married again."

Miriam appreciated their attempts to encourage her, but they didn't know the whole truth. They had no idea about Michael, the man she had loved out in the wilds of the desert where they both felt safe. Deep down she knew that even her loyal friends wouldn't be so kind if they knew she had dallied with a farmhand before she married Nirgal. It would be beyond their ability to comprehend, and they would probably never speak to her again. And Miriam was certain of one thing – she would rather leave and never see her friends again than tell them the truth and face their rejection. She could not bring herself to face the shame.

With arms linked, they walked on. Miriam's stride became more certain, and her spirits lifted when she saw an old man standing beside a donkey by the town gate. The donkey lapped water from a trough while the old man looked around myopically. Buoyed by her newfound confidence, Miriam went up to him. They haggled for a while, but finally settled on a reasonable fare.

"He says he knows Shechem well and will take me to my aunt's house," she told her friends. They gaped at her.

Mary was the first to recover. Looking the old man up and down, she said, "He looks worn out. Are you sure he'll make it?"

Miriam nodded. "I've seen him ferrying people along this road for years. I'll be okay."

Though his old legs were coated in dirt and his sandals were falling apart, his small eyes sparkled with quick intelligence. There was an air of confidence about him, and his sunburned hands held the donkey's reigns in a way that could only have come from years of working with the stubborn beasts. He peered at the women through thick eyebrows framed by wild grey hair, and asked rather too loudly, "You coming?"

Sheerah let out a nervous giggle. Mary nudged her sharply in the ribs. "Stop that."

Miriam sighed. "Here we go then."

She hugged each of her friends tightly. "You are good friends. You know I love you all. You are my sisters, and I will miss you all so much. Perhaps when you make your pilgrimage to Mt Gerizim your husbands will permit us to meet again?"

"Yes," they all agreed. "Let them try to stop us." Miriam remained stoic amid their tearful farewells. She did not want to appear vulnerable in front of the old man. She squared her shoulders, held her chin up and walked as confidently as she could towards her destiny.

The old man offered to help her up onto the donkey's back. "Thank you, but I would rather walk."

"Walk?" He sounded offended by the idea.

"Well at least for a while," Miriam didn't want to cause a fuss, but she knew she couldn't sit still with so many emotions churning around inside her.

The old man shrugged his shoulders. "The beast will be pleased, I guess," he huffed and turned to leave. "But you better keep up or I'll make you climb up."

"Fair enough," Miriam nodded.

No further words were spoken. Miriam walked beside the old man, down the road and away from Sychar. She turned and waved to the huddled shape of her friends but did not allow a single tear to fall until the sun had sunk low on the horizon. Her heart ached with loss and fear. Would she ever see Sychar again? And did she even want to?

Chapter XI

Open The Book

Mount Gerizim stands at a height of
881 m (2,890 ft) above sea level.
It was the original Holy Place of the Israelites from the
time that Joshua conquered Canaan and the tribes of Israel
settled the land.

Open the book and tell me your story.
Tell me through eyes that no one else sees.
You won't find any judgment here I promise,
As you unravel your history with me.
For where you describe a coward's failure,
I see the warrior who is willing to stand.
Where you remember the setbacks and mistakes,
I see you rising with open hands.
Where you carry bags of guilt and shame,
I say they no longer belong to you.
Where you feel the weight of judgement's fury,
I see you breaking it down to find breakthrough.
For where you see mountains of impossibility,
I see the first crack in the wall.
Where you've accepted defeat's conclusion,
I see your potential to rise and stand tall.
So, don't be afraid to let me see
The path that has led you here.
For if the way has been unstable,
Let it shake the dust from your fears.
Give yourself permission to live authentically,
And never mind who might disagree,
For if there's one thing I've learnt, it's that authenticity,
Is the only way to live free.

Miriam – age 26

Shechem's old sandstone houses rambled along the streets like pebbles tumbling down a stream. The place had a life and vibrancy that Miriam's hometown of Sychar did not possess.

Nestled in the shadow of the mighty Mount Gerizim, Shechem hosted people from across the country during holy festivals. It further flourished due to its idyllic location at the heart of Israel, and local merchants thrived by supplying the needs of the constant stream of weary travellers making their annual pilgrimage to the mountain. Markets, filled with the delicious aroma of freshly baked goods, colourful fruits, handmade artifacts, livestock and religious trinkets all lined the streets.

Miriam loved the hustle and bustle of everyday life in the town. She felt free for the first time in many years. Here, she could blend into the mass of unknown people who filled the city. She relished the feeling of being able to walk through the markets and up into the foothills that fringed the town without being recognised, judged or pitied as she had been in Sychar. The air felt clear and clean. She could finally breathe again.

The Samaritans believed Yahweh would one day build a Holy Temple on Mount Gerizim and held sacred rituals on the mount three times a year. The Jews, however, believed that the location of the chosen place to worship was the Temple Mount of Moriah in Jerusalem. The disagreement over the significance of Mount Gerizim became a source of conflict between the two groups.

Although Miriam had rebelled against the religious doctrines her father brandished like rods of iron, she could not deny that Mount Gerizim was awe inspiring. Breathtaking in its sheer size and splendour, the aura of holiness about Mount Gerizim gave her a sense of both wonder and peace. Miriam's growing confidence took her further into the foothills each time she ventured out. She loved to watch over the town and the valley from high up. It made her troubles seem far away.

Miriam had been pleasantly surprised by the welcome her aunt had bestowed on her. Her unannounced arrival had come at just the right time, for Aunt Ellan sorely needed help. And, six months after Miriam's arrival, in the strange quiet that always settles in an aftermath of conflict, she finally found a modicum of peace and the inkling of a new beginning.

Like her mother, Miriam's aunt was refreshingly forthright, with a good sense of humour and a quick wit. She held her faith close but did not dogmatically level it at others. Ellan moved through society by holding it all lightly. Although she was a relatively wealthy and respected woman, she had a wide social circle that included friends and acquaintances from all social castes and religions within Shechem.

She had been widowed at a young age and had never remarried. She was a seamstress of legendary skill and a favourite among the town's wealthiest women.

Ellan had dressed many townsfolk for their wedding days. She also often made clothing and carried out alterations for women who could not afford her services, without expecting anything in return.

It was this same generous heart that had welcomed Miriam into her home. Though she was grateful for Miriam's assistance, Aunt Ellan did not overburden her with work, and in so doing, gave Miriam the time and space she needed to heal from her trauma and grief.

"You know, it took me a long time to admit to myself that I was having any trouble with my hands," she said one day. "I just wouldn't let myself believe it." Ellan shook her head sadly and stared out of the window. The view was quite spectacular. From their vantage point on the side of a small hill, they could see clear across the town's bustling central square to the blue foothills in the distance. Mt Gerizim rose glorious and mysterious from among them. The holy mount was truly awesome to behold, particularly in the early hours of the morning when a thick white cloud of mist fell gently down its sides.

Miriam followed her gaze, and they both kept their eyes on the mountain as her aunt continued, "I didn't want to acknowledge it, even though the pain was waking me up at night. I could not think of losing the one thing I really need for my work. How could I become crippled in my hands? So, I ignored it, but it would not go away. Eventually, I paid the priests to make sacrifices at the temple and say healing prayers on my behalf. Of course it was to no avail. When I lost the use of my hands, I could no longer afford servants, and this made managing the house very hard. My friends helped for a while, but they have their own duties to tend to, so I was left to struggle on my own. After months of agony, in desperation, I consulted some of the healers in town."

"Surely, they could do something for you?"

Aunt Ellan stared down at her hands. "No. They say it's a twisting of the bones. They don't know why it happens, and there is no cure. They gave me an herbal balm that used to sometimes ease the pain, but after a while even this treatment no longer worked."

Miriam felt a heavy sadness for her aunt. If not for the disfiguring bone twisting disease, she would be running rings around the socialites of Shechem even in her older years. Ellan still kept a gnarled finger on the pulse of the town and knew the gossip about everyone in it. Miriam enjoyed her tales. Ellan had them all pegged and labelled, just like the clothes they wore.

But today, Miriam sensed a vulnerability that her aunt seldom showed.

"For many long years," said Ellan. "I've been hoping and praying for a miracle. Eventually, all the hoping and longing for healing exhausted me, and I gave in to despair. I thought that my miracle would never come. Now, I see it has come, just not in the form of healing."

"What do you mean?"

"It's you, my dear. You are my miracle. Your

presence here has not only eased my burden, it has reconnected me with a part of my family I thought had been lost forever. You are so much like your mother, Miriam. It warms my heart to have you here." The two women were silent for a long time, each remembering Miriam's mother in their own way.

"You're my miracle, Aunt Ellan. I never dared to expect such a warm welcome after arriving on your doorstep unbidden and unannounced. I don't know where I would have ended up if you hadn't let me stay with you."

"Praise God, we have been able to help each other. I haven't asked what brought you here as it's none of my business, but knowing your father as I do, I can only imagine that you haven't had the easiest time since your mother passed and you were pressured to marry."

Miriam withdrew into her shame like a thief into the shadows. "It's been hard," she murmured.

"Well, here's what I know," Ellan's voice raised slightly as she spoke. "Matters of the heart can never be controlled by the letters of the law. The heart is much too complicated and wilful to be trapped by the black and white binds of religious duty. And you can take that on good authority – I've seen it all my dear. Every drama, love triangle and scandalous affair you can imagine. They have all walked into my shop over the years. Women need other women to talk to, and I'm not one to judge, so they tend to talk openly to me."

Miriam felt relief flood through her being. Someone

understood. Should she open up to Ellan? Unburden herself at last? But Ellan went on, "However my dear, you must be very careful whom you talk to. Don't open your heart up to just anyone, for some will turn on you faster than you can turn a shekel over in your hand. And sometimes friends may prove to be as fickle as foes."

Miriam considered her aunt's words. "To be honest, I don't talk to anyone," she admitted.

"Well, if you ever need a compassionate ear, I have two. And I will never disclose your secrets to anyone."

"Thank you." They sat in companionable silence a while longer watching the sandstone buildings change colour in the light of the setting sun.

"Do you know much about the history of Shechem?" Ellan asked.

"No, I suppose I don't. Not really."

"It has, at times, been a place of terrible trouble and sorrow."

"Really?" Miriam looked out at the streets that seemed so peaceful in the late afternoon sun.

"Yes. In the days of the judges, there was a man called Abimelech who was not one to give people much freedom. He became ruler here right after Gideon, who was known as a man of God that brought peace and prosperity to the land. Gideon was a favourite amongst the Israelites, but after Gideon's death, Abimelech moved to Shechem and convinced the people that he should be their ruler."

"And what happened?"

"The prophet Jotham warned the Israelites that Abimelech would not be a good leader, but they didn't listen. We're all the same, I guess, no matter how many generations pass. We seldom listen to good advice. We all think we know what's best. Would you like me to tell you the story?" Ellan got up, walked over to a shelf on the wall, and pulled down a heavy scroll. Painstakingly, she unravelled it.

"Yes, very much."

"Well, when Jotham heard about Abimelech's intentions, he climbed to the top of Mount Gerizim. He shouted from there, 'Listen to me, citizens of Shechem! Listen to me if you want God to listen to you!'

'Once upon a time the trees decided to choose a king. First, they said to the olive tree, "Be our king!" But the olive tree refused, saying, "Should I quit producing the olive oil that blesses both God and people, just to wave back and forth over the trees?"

'Then they said to the fig tree, "You be our king!" But the fig tree also refused, saying, "Should I quit producing my sweet fruit just to wave back and forth over the trees?"'

'Then they said to the grapevine, "You be our king!" But the grapevine also refused, saying, "Should I quit producing the wine that cheers both God and people, just to wave back and forth over the trees?"'

'Then all the trees finally turned to the thornbush

and said, "Come, you be our king!" And the thornbush replied to the trees, "If you truly want to make me your king, come and take shelter in my shade. If not, let fire come out from me and devour the cedars of Lebanon.'"

"Jotham continued, 'Now make sure you have acted honourably and in good faith by making Abimelech your king, and that you have done right by Gideon and all of his descendants. Have you treated Gideon with the honour he deserves for all he accomplished? For he fought for you and risked his life when he rescued you from the Midianites. But today you have revolted against my father and his descendants, killing his seventy sons on one stone. And you have chosen his slave woman's son, Abimelech, to be your king just because he is your relative.'

'If you have acted honourably and in good faith toward Gideon and his descendants today, then may you find joy in Abimelech, and may he find joy in you. But if you have not acted in good faith, then may fire come out from Abimelech and devour the leading citizens of Shechem and Beth-millo; and may fire come out from the citizens of Shechem and Beth-millo and devour Abimelech!'

Then Jotham escaped and lived in Beer because he was afraid of his brother Abimelech." Aunt Ellen paused and looked over at her niece.

"I'm not really sure I understand," Miriam confessed.

"The prophet Jotham warned the people that they

were making a mistake. God did not want Israel to have a king over them. He wanted them to serve Him only. Jotham knew the Israelites had not honoured Gideon. In fact, Abimelech had also murdered Gideon's sons to take power for himself. Listen to what happened next.

You see, after Abimelech had ruled over Israel for three years, God sent a spirit that stirred up trouble between Abimelech and the leading citizens of Shechem, and they revolted.

God was punishing Abimelech for murdering Gideon's seventy sons, and the citizens of Shechem for supporting him in this treachery of murdering his brothers.

The citizens of Shechem set an ambush for Abimelech on the hilltops and robbed everyone who passed that way. But someone warned Abimelech about their plot.

One day, Gaal son of Ebed moved to Shechem with his brothers and gained the confidence of the leading citizens of Shechem. And during the annual harvest festival at Shechem, held in the temple of the local god, the wine flowed freely, and everyone began cursing Abimelech.

'Who is Abimelech?' Gaal shouted. 'He's not a true son of Shechem, so why should we be his servants? He's merely the son of Gideon, and this Zebul is merely his deputy. Serve the true sons of Hamor, the founder of Shechem. Why should we serve Abimelech? If I were in charge here, I would get rid of Abimelech. I would say to him, 'Get some soldiers, and come out and fight!'

But when Zebul, the leader of the city, heard what

Gaal was saying, he was furious. He sent messengers to Abimelech in Arumah, telling him, 'Gaal son of Ebed and his brothers have come to live in Shechem, and now they are inciting the city to rebel against you. Come by night with an army and hide out in the fields. In the morning, as soon as it is daylight, attack the city. When Gaal and those who are with him come out against you, you can do with them as you wish.'

So, Abimelech and all his men went by night and split into four groups, stationing themselves around Shechem. Gaal was standing at the city gates when Abimelech and his army came out of hiding.

When Gaal saw them, he said to Zebul, 'Look, there are people coming down from the hilltops!' Zebul replied, 'It's just the shadows on the hills that look like men.'

But again, Gaal said, 'No, people are coming down from the hills. And another group is coming down the road past the Diviners' Oak.'

Then Zebul turned on him and asked, 'Now where is that big mouth of yours? Wasn't it you that said, "Who is Abimelech, and why should we be his servants?" The men you mocked are right outside the city! Go out and fight them!'

So Gaal led the leading citizens of Shechem into battle against Abimelech. But Abimelech chased him, and many of Shechem's men were wounded and fell along the road as they retreated to the city gate.

Abimelech returned to Arumah, and Zebul drove Gaal and his brothers out of Shechem.

The next day, the people of Shechem went out into the fields to battle. When Abimelech heard about it, he divided his men into three groups and set an ambush in the fields. When Abimelech saw the people coming out of the city, he and his men jumped up from their hiding places and attacked them.

Abimelech and his group stormed the city gate to keep the men of Shechem from getting back in, while Abimelech's other two groups cut them down in the fields.

The battle went on all day before Abimelech finally captured the city. He killed the people, levelled the city, and scattered salt all over the ground.

When the leading citizens who lived in the tower of Shechem heard what had happened, they ran and hid in the temple of Baal-berith. Someone reported to Abimelech that the citizens had gathered in the temple, so he led his forces to Mount Zalmon. He took an axe and chopped some branches from a tree, then put them on his shoulder. 'Quick, do as I have done!' he told his men.

So, each of them cut down some branches, following Abimelech's example. They piled the branches against the walls of the temple and set them on fire. So, all the people who had lived in the tower of Shechem died – about 1,000 men and women.

Then Abimelech attacked the town of Thebez and captured it.

But there was a strong tower inside the town, and all the men and women – the entire population – fled to it.

They barricaded themselves in and climbed up to the roof of the tower. Abimelech followed them to attack the tower, but as he prepared to set fire to the entrance, a woman on the roof dropped a millstone that landed on Abimelech's head and crushed his skull.

He quickly said to his young armour bearer, 'Draw your sword and kill me! Don't let it be said that a woman killed Abimelech!' So, the young man ran him through with his sword, and he died. When Abimelech's men saw that he was dead, they disbanded and returned to their homes. In this way, God punished Abimelech for the evil he had done against his father by murdering his seventy brothers."

"All those people were murdered in Shechem?"

"Yes," Ellan knew the story like she had grown up on it. "We have a sad history, but we choose not to live in the past. Well, we try. Instead of looking backwards, we have to keep moving forward. One day and one hour and one minute at a time."

Miriam smiled and nodded to convey her understanding of this lesson. Just like the people of Shechem, she could choose to let go of her own past and move on. She wanted to ask, "But how?" Instead, she asked, "But what if history repeats?"

"Then we live the same desctruction all over again. But if we learn from the past and make different decisions next time around, we don't have to reap the same consequences."

Miriam spent a lot of her free time walking in the foothills around Mount Gerizim. She pondered the stories Aunt Ellan told her and tried to imagine what it would have been like to live and die in the brutal days of Abimelech.

Mount Gerizim was said to be the highest and most central mountain in the world, the northern side was steep and imposing and trails converged on the gentler southern slope.

Miriam had been to the mountain as a child on a Passover pilgrimage and had found the sacred rituals both fascinating and terrifying. The mountain was considered sacred for many reasons. There were many other religious stories associated with the mountain. It was here, Abraham had taken his son Isaac as a sacrifice to the Lord, and Moses had exhorted the people to worship the Lord.

Now, Miriam tried to imagine Abraham and his son scrambling up the sides of the mountain. She wondered what Isaac must have thought when his father began to tie him to the altar. Did he scream and beg for his life or was he resigned and hopeless by the time he realised what was going on? Did he think his father had lost his mind?

She couldn't help wondering what might have happened if the ram in the bush had not provided Abraham with a way out. Would he really have killed his own son? And how would Sarah receive the news that her only son had been sacrificed? Would she have gone mad?

In the end, Miriam decided it was best to stop asking questions she would never know the answer to. She was glad the story had ended the way it had. God had met man's devotion with mercy and provided the ram instead. That was that.

Miriam realised she had been doing the same with her own life. Filling her thoughts with a constant cycle of 'what if' questions. What if Caleb had not died? What if she'd had children with Nirgal? What if she had never let Michael do those things…

Now she realised that all these questions were pointless. There was only what had been and what was to come. So far, in spite of her great failures, God had met her with mercy, and she was thankful.

Chapter XII

Discontent

Samaritans call themselves Shamerim, meaning guardians, or watchers. They see themselves as keepers of the holy law which is the one truth that has not been corrupted.

Wanting what I do not have
Craving all that is not mine.
Seeking after what is lost
Missing what I cannot find.

Needing more than I can hold
Searching for what is not there.
Hunting for another truth
Never playing fair.

This is the way of discontent
This is the path to deep dis-ease.
The unappreciated life
That will bring you to your knees.

For always getting your own way
And taking what is not your own
Is to rip out life's most fragile beauty
And plant weeds into your soul.

To simply take and take and take
Will leave you empty and bone dry.
Always craving more
But never being satisfied.

Man cannot live
By materialistic greed alone
And to grow bounty in your soul
Is to often tell it, "No".

Miriam – age 27

She sensed him before she saw him. An uncanny feeling that she was being watched crept slowly up her spine. Their eyes met through the rows of fruit and colourful spices. His were deep brown and twinkled with mischief. He smiled and winked at her. Miriam's heart skipped a beat. She snapped her gaze away and moved quickly onto the next stall. She picked up a pomegranate and turned it over, inspecting the red skin for blemishes.

"Locally grown in the hills behind Shechem," said the storekeeper without being asked. "The freshest you'll find. Our family has been growing and selling fruit for generations. Oldest stall in the market. We look after the people of Shechem. Give you best prices."

The old woman gave Miriam a snaggle-toothed smile, and Miriam wondered whether the storekeeper ever got tired of that well-worn spiel – no doubt repeated multiple times a day. She passed the pomegranate over to the woman, "How about this one?"

"Ah. A good one, for sure." The woman eyed the large red fruit in Miriam's hand. Then she picked up another which, to Miriam's untrained eyes, looked exactly the same as the one she had chosen. "But look, this one is even better." The woman ran her calloused, stained fingers over the fruit's plump ruby skin. "This one has no dents or blemishes. Like you my dear. A beautiful fruit picked at just the right time."

Miriam blushed at the strange and awkward compliment.

"Shalom." The deep voice startled her. "Excuse my asking, but have you ever been compared to a ripe pomegranate before?" Miriam turned to see those dark brown eyes staring at her, evidently delighting in her discomfort. Now she could see him properly, she noticed that he was a soldier.

'I, um … no." Shocked by his effrontery, she hurriedly replaced the fruit and walked quickly away. Her aunt had warned her often about the soldiers and their charming ways, but with each warning, Miriam had thought of her first husband. Caleb had been a soldier and she had never once had reason to doubt his integrity.

Still, better safe than sorry, she thought as she hastened away. She heard him behind her, shouting, "Miss, wait. I'm sorry I didn't mean to upset you." Against her better judgement, she stopped and turned to face him. He stood in the middle of the road with a disarming smile spreading across his face.

Rivetted to the spot by the intensity of his gaze, she felt like a mouse pinned down by a hungry cat. She turned her head and tried to move again, but he had caught up with her, and now his broad chest and broader shoulders blocked her path in the busy marketplace.

"I apologise for my rudeness, but surely, you can't blame me? You are truly the most beautiful woman I've ever seen." She said nothing, only kept her eyes downcast.

"I'm Alexander."

"I have to go." Miriam tried to keep her voice steady. "Please step aside."

"At least, tell me your name?"

"My name is Miriam," she said primly. "Now, please get out of my way."

"With pleasure, Miriam," he said and stepped aside with a flourish.

She felt his eyes on her as she made her way through the crowd to the sanctuary of her aunt's house.

"You've been distant over the last few days Miriam. What's on your mind?"

"Oh nothing," she lied, knowing full well that she had been preoccupied with thoughts of the soldier she had met in the marketplace.

He had been as unwelcome as a fly on a dinner plate, yet she could not stop wondering about him. What was it about him that she found so fascinating? Those eyes? That smile? His audacious nature? Surely not the ridiculous compliments he had showered on her? She had no idea. All she knew was that he had managed to get through her defences and crack open a door in her heart that she thought she had closed for good. It was just a crack, but it was enough.

Every time her duties took her back to the market, she had kept an eye out for him. This infuriated her, but she was powerless to stop herself. It had already become a habit. Like biting your nails, she thought. I'll never be able to stop. Her heart seemed intent on carrying her off in the wrong direction again. When would it ever learn?

"I think I may get out and go for a walk later today if that's alright with you. Some fresh air is probably what I need."

"Of course, my dear," her aunt replied. "I know how you love being out in nature. It's good to be able to find joy in this world, and even better to find something that truly satisfies your soul."

"Does anything every truly satisfy? I mean really?"

Ellan paused a moment before answering. "Well, I guess it must be God, mustn't it?"

"I guess. I do love being out in the wild. And I feel closer to God out there than I ever have in any temple. But I always have to come back down to earth where I can't sense His presence anymore."

"I can understand that. I wish I had the answer for you. Wouldn't it be wonderful if there was a way that we could all stay connected to God all the time, no matter where we were?" They both remained silent for a while. Then Ellan said, "I guess, I found my connection through my creativity. God loves to create and I think that's why He gave us the ability to create beautiful things, like the garments I used to make for the women of Shechem. I guess that's why my work always fulfilled me. It brought me closer to Him." Then she added, "Why don't you go now and spend some time on the mountain? Just don't forget to take some food and water and be back before dark."

"But it's not even lunchtime. How will you cope all afternoon without me?"

"Oh, you worry too much. I'll be fine. Off you go."

"Thank you, Aunt Ellan. I'll make you some lunch

before I go." Miriam put together a tray of flat bread, dried meat, olives, dates, salt and fresh olive oil. Delivering it to Ellan, she kissed the top of her aunt's curly head before hurrying out of the house.

Miram ran until she came to a field of wildflowers. She collected bunches of the multi-coloured treasures, until she could carry no more. Their colourful faces reminded her of happy days spent with her mother.

Life had been so much simpler when she was young. She longed to ask her mother's advice about many things in life, although she already knew what her mother would say about Alexander. She could hear the words clearly in her head. "Stay away from him Miriam. He will only bring you trouble."

Pushing these thoughts aside, she sat contentedly in the middle of the field and watched tiny birds dart in and out of the long grasses. Bees buzzed around the flowers, humming as they collected pollen. Miriam watched them intently – marvelling at their intricate movements, and the way their furry little backsides stuck precariously out of each bloom. It seemed miraculous that a tiny bee could know its purpose so thoroughly.

If a bee can understand its role in this world and find its way, why can't I? She lay back and closed her eyes against the glare of the afternoon sun.

"God, please help me," she prayed. "I feel so lost sometimes. So alone. Please protect me from my own heart. I don't want it to run away with me again." She had no idea whether God was listening. After a while, she got up and headed back into town.

The dusty streets were a checkerboard of colour, and the market was loud and crowded with men and women haggling for wares. Miriam pushed her way towards the temple. As she got closer to the gates, she noticed a change in the produce on offer. Fruit stalls morphed into animal stalls selling sacrificial beasts that could be presented at the temple. Chickens, sheep, goats, calves and pigeons were all on offer, if you had the money.

Miriam had to search for one she could afford. A small one would have to do. Her whispered prayers would blow away with the wind unless she could find a suitable sacrifice to atone for her sins.

After a while she spied a little white dove that seemed to have no marks or blemishes. She hoped it would be enough for God to hear her plea. The sad and scared bird in a cage by itself reflected her own feelings of fear and isolation perfectly.

Miriam decided this dove would be her small but spotless offering. Her only assurance that her prayers would be heard by the Almighty. She haggled over the price and eventually agreed upon two shekels for the bird.

The storekeeper handed it to her, and Miriam clutched the bird to her chest. She could feel its small heart beating wildly. Suppressing the sadness she felt over its premature death and resisting the urge to simply set it free, she headed straight for the crowded temple steps.

Miriam joined the noisy and chaotic crowd waiting to make their sacrifices. One by one, they handed their protesting and bewildered animals to the priests before being ushered into the outer chamber of the temple sanctuary. Only those who offered a sacrifice as payment were permitted inside.

Miriam wondered about the many reasons these people had come to petition God. One woman was wailing, carrying the limp form of a small child in her arms. A man had his arm protectively around her shoulders, and they walked in together. There was no need to guess at their request.

When she reached the front of the line, Miriam gently handed the dove over to the priest. She felt the soft feathers slip beyond the end of her fingertips into the priests wrinkled old hands. Then it was gone. She forced a smile, hoping that the priest would be pleased with her gift, but he didn't acknowledge her. He took the bird and passed it to someone just out of sight. Then he waved her through, his eyes already fixed upon the next animal in the line.

The outer chamber of the temple was just as crowded as the steps outside had been. People knelt in fervent prayer, lost in their own private thoughts, desperate to exchange their pain for hope. She saw the couple with the child and moved away from them, unable to face the raw grief etched on their faces. She searched for some small space where she might be alone with her thoughts and find some connection to the Almighty. Eventually, she headed to a far corner at the front of the chamber. With her back to the crowd, she could focus better.

She knelt and gazed up at the arched ceiling. Light streamed in from small high windows. A shiver went up her spine at the thought that she might actually be in the presence of Yahweh. She had been to the temple in Sychar many times during her marriage to Nirgal, beseeching God to open her womb and allow her to conceive a child. But when no child had been given to her, Miriam had silently concluded no sacrificial animal would ever be enough to atone for her sins. Why would God listen to a woman like her? She was far too sinful for God to even look upon, let alone bless.

Now, as she stood at the front of the sanctuary again, she wondered whether anything had changed. Yet, despite her doubts, she bowed her head and tried to pray. Thoughts and whispered words, came out in fragments, along with her tears.

"I am a sinful woman … I am wicked … to the core. You know my many sins, Oh Lord. And You know my heart is a wild horse that I cannot control. Please cleanse me and take away these thoughts of this soldier. Let me be content just as I am. If … if by some miracle, you should give me another husband one day, please let it be someone I can love? Someone who is kind and good and loves me.

Please let us have children and be a family. Let me be the type of woman my mother would have been proud of. Please help me not to bring further disgrace to my father's name."

After a while, Miriam wiped away her tears. She looked around and saw the couple from the steps, wailing now over their lifeless child. She sucked in her breath and hurried away, hoping against hope that God had heard her request amidst all the others.

Outside, the sunlight blinded Miriam. She held onto the smooth stone pillar with one hand and shielded her brow with the other giving her eyes a chance to adjust. It was just then that she sensed someone close to her and was shocked when she recognised Alexander.

"Miriam," he nodded and smiled.

Miriam could make no reply. Was God mocking her? Had he ignored her prayers? Desperate to go, but wanting to stay, she settled on the wisest course of action, nodded politely and quickly walked away. "Wait," he called after her.

Reluctantly, she stopped and turned to face him.

"I … I wanted to apologise to you. Properly this time."

She held his gaze, feeling her face flush. "Well, go on," she said with a confidence that surprised her.

"I was forthright and … well rude, I guess. I mean, I should not have said those things to you."

"Apology accepted." She stuck her chin up a little

higher. "Now, I really must get home." Deciding to keep her feet firmly on the moral high ground, she turned and walked away. She did not look back, and he did not follow her. Perhaps God had heard her prayers after all.

However, when she reached her aunt's house, Alexander was waiting for her beside the front door. Exasperated and a little daunted by his sudden appearance, she demanded, "What are you doing here? I accepted your apology, and I have nothing further to say to you. Good evening." She tried to get past him, but those broad shoulders once more blocked her way.

"Will you not give me the chance to get to know you?"

"No."

"Please, Miriam?" His eyes were very dark and very round. She felt she could get lost in those eyes.

"Miriam," Aunt Ellan called down from her vantage point beside the window.

He smiled, "Is that your aunt?"

"Yes."

"I would like meet her. If you don't mind. Let her be the judge of my true worth."

Miriam laughed. "Okay, if you promise to leave me alone when she doesn't approve. You should know my aunt disapproves of soldiers—"

"I'm a captain."

"It will make no difference. Besides, I'm a good Samaritan woman. We don't go around with strange men –

no matter whether they are captains or not."

"I'm not a stranger, you already know my name. I'm from Joppa, so now you also know my origins."

"But you're not a Samaritan. You're not even a Jew."

"My mother was a Jew, though my father was not. It's unusual yes, but not unheard of, and they made it work."

Miriam recalled her own mixed heritage and hesitated.

"Miriam, it's time to come inside," Ellan called again. Miriam jumped.

"Coming," she called back. Then more quietly to Alexander, "I really have to go now." Aunt Ellan's face disappeared from the window, but Miriam knew she would still be watching and trying to listen to their conversation.

Alexander was undaunted. "Meet me tomorrow morning. I'll wait for you by the fruit seller. You know the one." She blushed at the memory.

"Okay," she conceded. Anything to get him to leave. "But I really must go in now."

"Miriam?" She heard barely disguised mirth in his voice and turned back with a scowl.

"What now?" She asked through gritted teeth.

"Thank you." And with that Alexander walked back down the street, waving up to Aunt Ellan as he went. Miriam watched him go. He was unlike anyone she had ever met before, and he filled her with a strange mixture of irritation, admiration and excitement.

Chapter XIII

Stir Me Up

Joppa was an important seaport in ancient Israel. Located within the tribal land of Dan on its border with Ephraim, one of the Samaritans' ancestral homelands, it lay between Caesarea and Gaza. It was situated about 30 miles northwest of Jerusalem, but only became a Jewish town in the second century B.C.

Oh, how you stir me up
From the bedrock of my soul.
You remind me of the things that matter,
Like I'm a wayward child you're calling home.
I'm the one who ran away
And now is lost
Out there somewhere.
The one who can't
Find solid ground
And is sinking deep into despair.
But I hear you calling clear,
Like soft drum beats
Over distant hills.
You call me to return to you,
And only there
Will I be filled.
The Captain of my salvation
Perfected in Your suffering.
The One who sanctifies His children,
To gather up and gather in.
The One
Who is not ashamed,
To call me one of Your own.
The One
Who is mighty to save,
And call every wayward child back home.
You do not give aid
To angels,
Yet You are here
To show me the way.
Your footsteps light the darkness
To bring the lost
Back home to stay.

Miriam – age 28

lexander had reeled her in like a fish, one tiny twist of the line at a time. One question at a time, he had made her doubt her own convictions. One statement at a time, he had contradicted everything she believed. Her faith and traditions, already resting upon shaky foundations, fractured and fell apart beneath Alexander's cynical scrutiny.

She was no match for his wit and charm. One smile. One wink. One small touch of his hand against hers.... She was vulnerable – and though she did not know it, Alexander did. He told her things she longed to hear. He said he loved her and always would. He said he would protect her and look after her always. That he wanted only her.

When he painted elaborate pictures of their life together and a home in Joppa, beside the sea, it had been more than her fragile defences could handle.

She saw him as inquisitive and funny, caring and constantly charming – a light in the darkness of her fears. A free spirit, he was unafraid to ask why, and he encouraged her to do the same. Alexander was the first person she had ever met who told her she could be free. The ancient customs were created by men who sought to control her, he said. Miriam jumped at the chance to be rid of the strict religious regulations of Samaritan society.

She fell for him so completely that, within a matter of months, nothing else really seemed to matter anymore.

Nothing but him. It didn't even seem to matter that he wasn't a Samaritan. He became her everything. She felt she needed him like she needed air. She laid all of her hopes and dreams at his feet, and she told him all about her sinful past. She thought it might push him away, but instead, he listened to her story and promised her that it only made him love her more. After that confession, he treated her more fondly and became more protective. Miriam didn't understand why, but she believed him. He offered the unconditional love she longed for and thought she might never find.

The only thing she did not tell him about was her relationship with Michael. To tell Alexander about that seemed too risky at many levels, so she decided to keep that part of her life to herself.

When the relationship with Alexander finally came to Aunt Ellan's attention, she was furious and deeply wounded by Miriam's breach of her trust. "I thought you genuinely want to get your life back on the right track?" she said. "I took you in, cared for you as though you were my own child. Yet, you betrayed my trust Miriam. I warned you not to get involved with this … this … soldier, and you ignored my advice. I'm devastated. I want you to know that I am going to send a message to your father letting him know that you have been staying with me. I'm going to ask him to come here with all possible haste. Perhaps he can talk some sense into you."

The threat was too much for Miriam. She knew

she could not go back, so she arranged to meet Alexander at midnight on the night before her father was due to arrive. Their plans to elope both excited and terrified her. There was a deep sense of guilt and loss now that she was leaving Aunt Ellan's shelter. She had left a message with a neighbour's servant girl, telling her to let Ellan know that she was safe, and that she and Alexander would marry and return to see her when the time was right.

As she crept from the house beneath the light of the silvery moonlight, she felt like a child again. Her heart raced inside her chest. When fear threatened to surface, she reminded herself that, as Alexander said, she had a right to choose the path her life would take. So, why then was she escaping in the dead of night? She pushed the question from her mind and focussed on the wonderful new life Alexander had promised her. She hurried towards the lane on the outskirts of town where he would be waiting.

There he was, standing silhouetted in the moonlight. His arms ready to embrace her. She threw herself into his embrace. "You're here."

"You came," he replied. Miriam wanted to linger under the soft shower of his kisses, feeling his heartbeat against her chest, but there was no time. Someone might see them, and besides, it was a long ride to Joppa. Sensing her nervousness, Alexander cupped her face in both hands. He smiled in the dark, and she felt his lips on hers. They shared one final lingering kiss.

"Are you ready my love?" She nodded, the lump

in her throat preventing her from making any sound. Alexander had told her so many wonderful stories about Joppa, the town by the sea, where he had grown up. She could not wait to meet his family, who he promised would love her as he did. And she was excited to see the ocean, and discover the treasures he said lay along the shore.

Perhaps in Joppa she would finally enjoy the life of freedom, excitement and adventure she had always longed for. Giving up the life she had known, one of religious obligation and servitude, seemed a surprisingly easy choice to make with Alexander. She would be a fool to refuse all that life with him offered. He put his strong hands around her waist and lifted her onto his horse, then jumped up behind her. Miriam felt his chest at her back and pressed herself against him. He was strong and safe, like a lighthouse in a storm.

"Let's go," she said. And Alexander spurred the horse on towards Joppa.

Miriam fell in love with Joppa on the very first morning she saw it. From the window, she looked out to see vivid green trees, and in the distance, a deep blue streak that she realised must be the ocean. Birds sang in the garden and the sweet scent of spring drifted through the open window. She knew she would never get tired of this view.

After a few quiet minutes, a young girl entered the room.

"Hello," she said shyly, nodding in Miriam's direction.

"Good morning," she replied, trying to hide the awkwardness she felt. "Are you Cloe?"

"Yes. I'm Alexander's youngest sister. And you are Miriam. He has told us all about you. I'm pleased to meet you, Miriam. We are all very excited about the wedding. Mama had almost given up on Alexander ever settling down."

Miriam laughed. "Well, I can't wait to meet her properly and apologise for waking the household when we arrived last night."

"That's okay. Are you hungry? You've missed breakfast, but there is some food prepared for you. Come join us in the courtyard. That's where Mama is waiting. She's getting us all involved in the wedding preparations. There's a lot to do in a very little time as Alexander wants to get married as soon as possible."

Feeling a little sheepish for sleeping so late when everyone else was up and already busy, she pulled on her outer tunic and sandals. She tied her hair into her head scarf then smiled at Cloe.

"There. That will have to do."

"You look lovely. You're even prettier than Alexander said. Come on, it's this way."

Miriam followed the young girl out of the room and

into the courtyard. Doubts suddenly assailed her. *Was she doing the right thing? Would Alexander's family accept her?*

The house was not grand but was much larger than the home she had known as a child. It had an elegance in the details that came from a woman's touch. They walked through a doorway at the end of the corridor and into a large courtyard. A robust, red-faced woman whom she recognised from the night before as Gabriella, Alexander's mother, sat on a bench giving orders to a group of young women. She looked over as Miriam approached.

"Ah, there you are. Did you sleep well, my dear?" The woman held out both hands to greet Miriam.

"Yes, thank you," Miriam smiled, her fears ebbing away in the warmth of the greeting.

"Good, good, because there are many things we need to do. But first, you must eat. Cloe, go and bring the bread and barley soup from the storeroom. This girl needs to get some meat on her bones. Go Cloe, hurry." Gabriella gave orders like a queen bee and Cloe obeyed her without a word. Miriam fell silent as Alexander's mother fussed around her.

She hardly paused for breath. "Now, after you've eaten, we will show you around Joppa. On the way, we will visit the local seamstress. You know it's hard to pull a wedding off at such short notice, but I know her and she owes me a favour. She'll rush the dress for you. Oh, it is all rather exciting, isn't it dear? Of course, it will be just a quiet wedding – if that's possible with our family. What I mean is nothing too showy. Alexander explained that you have no family to invite. That's sad of course but coming into our family will more than make up for that. You know, we are a very large family here in Joppa. We've been here for many generations. There are cousins, uncles and aunties everywhere. It's something you will get used to. Keep eating, keep eating. Do you want water? Get some water, Cloe. You're probably parched from that long ride, and of course, Alexander wouldn't think to bring extra water. He can't concentrate, that boy. Always been his main problem. Ever since he was a boy, he just can't focus on what's right in front of him. It's a miracle he hasn't lost his own head by now."

A cup of water appeared in front of Miriam, and Cloe hissed at her mother under her breath, "Shhh, you're scaring her."

"Oh dear, it's alright. You know, I'm only teasing a bit. I do that, but you'll get used to it. We're just getting acquainted that's all." She slapped Miriam on the back almost making her spill her drink. Then to Cloe, "I want Miriam to feel as welcome as possible."

Seeing Miriam's untouched food, Gabriella added, "My, but you are a slow eater."

Feeling abashed, Miriam picked up a piece of bread and dipped it into the bowl of soup. It was delicious and made her realise how hungry she was. While she ate, Gabriella kept talking.

"Good, that's it. You eat up. Don't let me distract

you. But I wanted to tell you that you can call me 'Mother'. Even my husband calls me Mother, so it's what I'm used to. Sometimes, even locals from the town call me Mother too. I guess I do tend to mother everyone, I know. You'll get used to that too, I hope. Do you mind calling me Mother?"

Miriam had almost choked on her soup when the strange request was sprung upon her. How could she call Alexander's mother Mother? It somehow felt like a dishonour to her own mother's memory. As if she could replace her so easily.

"I … don't mean to be rude. But would you mind if I called you something else?"

"Something else? But everyone calls me mother."

"Mother," hissed Cloe. "Please stop it. It might not be something Miriam is comfortable with right now."

"Well, it's just that I lost my own mother and she was the only mother I have known. I don't know if I can call anyone else mother."

"Oh, my dear, of course. You mustn't. I do understand. That poor woman passed far too early and left a beautiful daughter behind. We will just have to think of something else. You can't very well call me Gabriella. Only my husband calls me that from time to time. But what about Aunty? Or Mother Gabby? What do you think dear?"

Miriam felt put on the spot and had once again completely forgotten her meal. "I … I'm sorry, I don't know."

"Oh. Well ok, let's just forget it for now my dear. I think over the next few days as you get to know me, you will figure out what's best. We will figure it out together."

"Thank you," replied Miriam, not quite sure whether she had just offended Alexander's mother. She wasn't sure what to make of the friendly and yet overbearing Gabriella. A tiny seed of doubt began to creep into the corner of her mind and settle there. Hardly noticeable, but present nonetheless, at the very outer reaches of her consciousness.

Pushing it down, Miriam closed her eyes and obligingly took another small bite of bread.

Over the coming weeks, as they all prepared for the wedding, Miriam noticed the strange glances between family members when they thought she wasn't looking. Occasionally, their hushed conversations would fall silent as soon as she walked into the room. She brushed her concerns aside with thoughts of waking up safely in the arms of the man she loved.

But she didn't have doubts, did she? Alexander felt right, didn't he? She wanted this to work. Wanted to be far enough away from her old life that even the memory of it would disappear. Their wedding day arrived, and all her doubts flew away when she felt Alexander's hand over hers. A thin white ribbon was tied around their palms, symbolically uniting them. It was done. She was once again a married woman.

Chapter XIV

Quiet Before The Storm

During the construction of Solomon's Temple, cedars were floated from Phoenicia to Joppa and then transported to Jerusalem (2 Chronicles 2:16).

Noleen Sanderson

In the quiet before the storm
There is a gathering,
Like all the earth holds her breath
And pulls her courage in.

There's a knowing
That the growing black
Hanging over darkened trees,
Is on its way
Unstoppable
To unleash on everything, it sees.

All preparations cease
As every small bird seeks a home.
A shelter from the coming wrath
That no creature can survive alone.

So they gather
And they hold
Cords invisible to man.
For nature knows how to survive,
And continue through each storm
To stand.

But if you listen to the quiet
Right before the test,
You will hear her drawing courage
As she holds her naked breath.

And in the violence
And the shaking
When no help is on the way,
She will rise above the darkness
And stand to see
Another day.

Miriam – age 29

Miriam lay alone on a small bamboo mat. A thick layer of dust had settled over the wooden kitchen utensils and bowls on the old shelf that hung on the opposite wall. Dust particles sifted down glinting in the morning sun. She dragged her eyes away from them and stared blankly at the empty water jug.

In her mind's eye, she was running through the foothills above her home in Sychar, carefree and blissfully lost in the wonder of the creation all around her. This simple picture revisited her often these days, connecting her by a thin cord of memory to the home she had once loved. The vision never lasted more than a few seconds, but it felt like a lifeline.

Alexander had moved her into the servants' shack soon after their wedding, and now they locked her in alone every night. Bewildered and afraid, she had wailed and cried out, to no avail. However, one morning in the second week, Cloe had appeared with a meal of bread and fruit, a wash basin and water and a clean tunic.

"Here, eat, wash and put this on. I'll wait outside." Miriam had hastily done as instructed. Cloe had taken her back to the big house where she presented her to Gabriella. The woman looked her up and down as though she had never laid eyes on her before and muttered, "Alexander is right, she's wasted on the slave block. Cloe she's yours now. Teach her all you know. I want her ready to present to customers within the month. Keep a close eye on her.

And you girl," she turned her gaze on Miriam. "You listen to Cloe and do as she says. One bit of trouble from you, and it's off to the slave market, you hear?" Miriam nodded, although the shock of her change in circumstance left her struggling to understand.

Cloe took Miriam under her wing. First she showed her how to dress and do her hair and make-up. Miriam could not help but marvel at the gawdy colours and outrageous clothes. Although there seemed an endless number of mannerisms and rituals to learn – everything from how to walk and talk properly through to the right way to pour wine – she was not burdened with any of the usual household chores. And at first, she felt relieved. Though she missed Alexander, Cloe was friendly enough.

Only when she asked Cloe what they were doing all this dressing up and parading around for, did she learn the awful truth.

"Why, to please Gabriella's customers of course. I thought you knew. You are naïve, aren't you? Haven't you got courtesans where you come from?"

"What? No!" So, Cloe explained to her that Gabriella's customers paid her large sums of money in exchange for spending the night with one of Gabriella's girls.

"They are wealthy men, and they take you to nice places, and sometimes, even buy presents. Although Gabriella always takes those for herself. Still, it's better than being sold on the slave market." Miriam did believe her, but it didn't make her feel any better. She did not want to go out with strange men and do who knew what with them. She consoled herself with the knowledge that she still had three weeks left of training before she would have to face her fate. She was mindful of Gabriella's threat and did her best to stay out of trouble.

Whenever her mind drifted to Alexander, his empty promises sat like bitter gall in the back of her throat. How stupid and naïve her dreams of having a life and a family with him now appeared. How could he have been a part of this awful deception? If only he would come back and prove that all her misgivings were wrong. Miriam worried that she might be driven crazy by her conflicting emotions.

As the days moved swiftly by, she gave up all hope of ever seeing Alexander again, and instead, her thoughts turned to escape. That was easier said than done.

That morning alone in the servants quarter, for the first time in a long time, Miriam got down on her knees and prayed. "Help me, God. Please help me to find a way out of this trap."

Miriam rose from her prayers and headed out into the courtyard. As she did so, she glimpsed Gabriella hurrying out of the gate. In her haste, she had forgotten to lock it. Miriam pulled a shawl from a hook beside the door and covering her face, she headed for the open gate. On the way over, she grabbed a basket. Today, she would be a slave no longer, just another woman on her way to market. Miriam kept her head down as she followed Gabriella. Her long legs made it easy to keep up with the large woman's shuffle.

Although early, the streets were already brimming with people. Women carrying water jugs and baskets made their way to the market, while children ran and played, and men talked to neighbours and friends. Miriam blended in easily, especially as they neared the market and the number of people increased. She had to be careful not to lose Gabriella around the various stalls.

Suddenly Miriam stopped and backed up, holding her breath. Gabriella had her back to her, but Miriam could see the man she was speaking to. He sat on a stool between two market stalls. His hair was longer and scruffy now, and a thick dark beard covered his chin. He was dressed in the manner common among the lower castes – brown tunic tied at the waist with a sash. But what struck her were his eyes. She would know those eyes anywhere. It was Alexander.

Miriam slowly let her breath out. Gabriella and Alexander were engaged in intense conversation for a while, then Gabriella passed him something small. Miriam could not make out what it was – perhaps a note, or money?

With that perfectly ordinary transaction, the last remaining facade of Miriam's world came crashing down. She could not move or take her eyes off the scene, and she stood in the shadows for a long moment, trying to make sense of what she had witnessed.

When Gabriella turned to leave, she walked straight

past Miriam. Her face was passive, businesslike and cold. That is not the look of a mother who had just found her son, Miriam thought. She looked at Alexander. Why is he here, dressed like that? What did she give him?

Filled with fiery anger, Miriam threw caution to the wind and stormed over to him. Alexander looked up at her, flashing his charming smile for an instant before recognising her. Shock wiped the smile away, but he replaced it with another in an instant.

"Hello Miriam," he said as if he were gentling a runaway mare.

"Hello Alexander." Her tone was stern and cold. He hung his head for an instant, then looked up at her sideways with a puppy dog expression that begged her to forgive him. She hardened her heart.

"What—" But before she could finish, he stood up and grabbed her by the elbow.

"Not here." He propelled her down a side alley and ushered her into a small doorway halfway along the wall. The room they entered was dim, and it took Miriam's eyes a moment to adjust after the bright morning sunlight. When they did, she saw that it was tiny with no windows and only an oil lamp for light. A sleeping mat lay on the floor in one corner of the room. Alexander's uniform hung from a hook on one wall. A shelf on the other side of the room, held a few oranges. Their vibrant skins glowed ethereally in the lamp light, making the rest of the room seem all the more soulless.

"Alexander? What is this place? What's going on? Why didn't you come home?" A tear slid down her cheek.

"Listen," he began. "I never wanted to hurt you. In the time I was with you, I became very fond of you. But I have to make a living."

"What are you talking about?" Miriam's mind whirled in confusion, trying to make sense of his words.

"Isn't it obvious Miriam? I work for Gabriella. Finding people, well mostly women, for her."

"Slaves, you mean?"

"Yes. But they are all hopeless cases, you know. People who have nowhere to go and no one to look out for them."

"But I did. I had my aunt, and …" She was going to say, "my father", but she was not sure of the truth of that.

Alexander looked down at his hands. She thought she saw a tiny flash of shame in his eyes?

"Yes, but you were beautiful, and Gabriella puts a high price on beautiful women. She has special plans for you as I'm sure you're already aware."

"Cloe has explained it all."

Miriam tried to leave, but he grabbed her.

"Wait. Where are you going?"

"As far away as possible from you, and Gabriella, and this whole awful mess."

"You can't."

"Just try to stop me." She jerked out of his grasp and grabbed the door handle.

"Stop. Gabriella's spies are everywhere. They will catch you as soon as you walk out of that door." He paused. "Look. I want to help you, Miriam. You're different from the other girls. I really like you—"

Miriam scoffed. "You have a strange way of showing it."

"I'm truly sorry. Since I left you, I haven't been able to get close to another girl. Gabriella has just given to me an ultimatum. If I don't get her a new girl soon, she'll cut me loose. I'll wind up in the desert with a knife in my back. Don't you see? If I can't work, I'm as good as dead."

Miriam didn't want to hear another word, yet, despite herself, she pitied what a pathetic excuse of a man he now seemed.

"It was a mistake to take you. I know that now. Please let me make this right?" he looked at her with such sincerity she almost believed him. Then she recalled how he had deceived her, and her anger rose once more.

"I'm going," she said. "Please get out of my way." Alexander strode up and down like a caged beast in front of the door. Pinching his nose between thumb and forefinger, he muttered recriminations to himself. She could make out only a few snippets of what he said, but foremost among them was, "I have displeased the gods."

How different this Alexander was from the one she had fallen in love with. Not the proud young son, or the captain in the army he had pretended to be. Not a handsome young man who longed for a wife and family as he'd claimed. Rather, what she saw was a broken, confused and superstitious soul, living in a dark dank room, plagued by guilt for what he had done to so many innocent women.

"What gods are you talking about?" she demanded.

"I'm not sure. But by taking you, I have brought bad luck upon myself. I must have displeased some god or other." He continued to rave. "Gabriella won't like it. But the gods need to be appeased." He looked up at her as though seeing her for the first time, "You." He looked directly at her face. "You must return to your own people."

"Yes, you're right," she said, seeing her opportunity. "It is my God whom you have displeased. He is angry that I have been taken from my home." As she said this, Miriam wondered if it was true. "My God is a jealous and vengeful God. If you don't help me escape and see me safely back to my people, you will lose everything. You must take me quickly back to my aunt's house."

"Yes, you're right. Your God and my gods must be appeased." He grabbed her by the shoulders. "You must wait here. I will get a horse and take you back to Shechem." He turned to the door.

"But it is bright daylight. Someone will see us."

He spun round, a long index finger pressed to his lips. "Oh." She could see his mind racing. "Then, what do we do? How do I get you home?"

"I could wait here until dark," she suggested, using a little of the charm Cloe had drummed into her. "You get the horse and supplies for the trip and come back here after dark. We'll leave tonight." She wanted to add, "like last time," but the memory stabbed her heart.

"Okay. You wait here, and I will go and make some arrangements." He said it as though it had been his idea all along and added unnecessarily, "Do not leave this house. Understand?"

Miriam nodded, surprised by the sudden change of tone in his voice. "I'll wait right here," she promised. He looked at her quizzically, so she added "I won't go anywhere. I have nowhere to go, remember?"

He nodded. "I'll be back as soon as I can."
Before he could open the door, she called out to him, "Oh, and one more thing Alexander. Don't go getting any ideas about turning me over to Gabriella. Remember, my God will rain down vengeance upon you if a single hair on my head is damaged." He paled at the thought and without another word he left.

Miriam made herself comfortable amongst the cushions that surrounded a low table and did her best to rest while she waited, but her stomach felt queasy and every noise that filtered through the door from the street, startled her. Time seemed to drag on interminably.

Eventually, she must have dozed off because she jumped awake when he opened the door. She could see the night sky beyond his head. It was time to go.

Chapter XV

Sitting In The Quiet

*The olive tree was an important part of life for ancient
Israelites. The trees grow to seven meters tall and live
for many years. Some olive trees in Israel are estimated to be
a thousand years old. They thrive in Israel's rocky,
well-drained soil and warm Mediterranean climate.
The tree continues to produce fruit long after its trunk has
become gnarled and hollow with age.*

Sitting in the quiet,
Waiting for a sign.
Letting go of everything
You have left behind.

And even though it's daunting
And the hardest cliff to climb,
You will come out shining
On the other side.

For you have faced giants before
And taken each one down.
This is just another test
To see if you will stand your ground.

So, wait here patiently
Wrapped up in perfect peace,
As you sit here in the silence
That is the quiet before release.

And when it's time to move
Hold your head up high,
For the Lord of all creation
Is right there by your side.

He goes before your every step.
So, hold tight to His hand.
He will never leave you,
And on His righteousness, you'll stand.

He puts the finishing touches
On each miracle He begins,
And you've already come so far
So don't lose sight of Him.

In every hour of darkness
Look only to His light,
For healing comes upon His wings
To lift you into flight.

Go now little warrior,
Gear yourself to move,
And tell your heart to just be brave
As you watch those giants loose.

Miriam – age 29

On the second day of her escape, Miriam slept late. When she finally awoke, she was startled to find the sun already high overhead. Oddly, the familiar sound of Alexander snoring nearby, was absent. Where was he?

"Alexander?" She sat up, initially assuming he was close. Perhaps he was seeing to the morning duty of camp pack up.

"Alexander?" she called a little louder. No reply except the birds chirping in a nearby tree.

"Alexander? Where are you?" Louder still.

Silence.

"Alexander! Answer me." Panic began to rise.

Miriam looked around wildly, trying to make sense of the scene, yet knowing instinctively that she was very much alone. Alexander was gone, as was his horse. The irony sunk in deep. In trusting him, he had once again, betrayed her.

Truth hit her like a shockwave. She had wanted to escape his presence, and yet had again become dependent upon him for protection in this facade of a journey.

Had he ever intended to take her home?

Had he ever wanted to help at all, or was he merely trying to dispose of his baggage in a way that made him look innocent?

Miriam stood up in the middle of their makeshift overnight camp and shouted up into the sky as loudly as she could.

"Alexander! Alexander!" Nothing. Only her echo followed by a deafening silence. It was the kind of silence that sent a sudden chill down her spine. Fear launched and she was immediately terrified. Without thinking she hid behind the trunk of a tree breathing heavily, cursing herself for shouting. Her mind raced as her body involuntarily shook. For a moment she couldn't move as fear rose and fell like waves tossed on a violent ocean. Logically she knew this level of fear was somewhat irrational, yet it felt so real. She found herself watching her body, as if from a distance, feeling completely out of control. She had been abandoned far enough away from any town that she knew she could be in real danger.

"Come on," she muttered under her breath, willing her body and mind to calm down and retain some sense of balance. "Breathe. Come on. Just breathe."

She closed her eyes tightly, hands clasped together pressing hard into her forehead as her body shook. Eventually the waves of anxiety subsided. Her mind raced as she stepped gingerly back towards the camp. She needed to properly assess the situation and figure out what to do.

Had he left her any food or water?

Alexander's belongings were gone. She shook her head at her own naivety, knowing she should have known better than to trust a man like him.

Why had she ever agreed that he could take her all the way back to Shechem?

Why had she not run when she had the chance?

Had she really thought he had some skerrick of love towards her that was real?

Was she really so foolish?

"This is my own fault," she told herself. Reason began to kick in. "I shouldn't be surprised, but did he have to take everything?"

Miriam was miles away from Shechem. They had ridden more than a day already but she didn't know the way or where she was. From here, it would be a long journey on foot and not safe for a woman to make alone.

She decided to move quickly and packed her own rations into her satchel, slung it over her shoulder and headed off down the path, walking out the overwhelming sense of fear and anger as she went.

After a few hours, Miriam finally slowed her pace to catch her breath, and it was then that she noticed the few scraggly olive trees she was passing under. They seemed to be cast offs from a thick grove that now flanked the road just up ahead on either side. Green olives peaked out between the leaves like jewels. The upper branches caressed each other forming a canopy over her head. Miriam was drawn off the road and into the protection of the leafy canopy. She found herself venturing into the grove.

Walking further away from the winding road, she eventually reached the summit of a small hill. Miriam breathed, as if for the first time. There was a safety in the trees. A feeling of being sheltered. Wanting a better vantage point, she threw the sachet to the ground and climbed the limbs of a sturdy olive tree. It forked towards the top and allowed her to stand and peak above the branches. From this position she could see down into the long valley that stretched out from Joppa in the west all the way over to the eastern horizon. Somewhere out there in the distance was Shechem and her aunt's home.

Would she be welcomed back or cast out?

Miriam suppressed the anxiety that again threatened to crash on her with such thoughts and looked over to the road that wound its way through farmlands into the valley. It lay quiet and deserted in the mounting heat of the day.

Miriam decided to take a break and gather her thoughts. She climbed down and sat with her back pressed into an ancient olive tree, the sun gently dappled and glinting through the branches above. After some minutes, she felt herself beginning to relax. Her hands kneaded the knots out of her aching feet and she allowed herself to nibble on a small piece of bread. This ration might have to last a while, and so, although she was hungry, she forced herself to eat slowly and sparingly.

"What are you doing here?" Miriam jumped at a man's voice behind her. She sprang to her feet and spun around to face the threat.

"Okay, take it easy now." A man stood before her. It was obvious from the way he was dressed that he was a farmer. He was handsome with a broad, honest, inquisitive face, and his hands were raised in mock surrender. An amused smile played at the corners of his mouth. "I'm Daniel. I mean you no harm. You're sitting beneath my olive trees is all. And we don't often see women alone in these parts. Are you lost?"

"I ah … I … No." She stumbled. "I just need to get home."

"Oh. And where is home?"

"Shechem."

He whistled in surprise before speaking. "That's a long way from here."

"Yes. But I need to get there."

"Well, why don't you come to my home? You can wash up, and my wife will make sure you get a bite to eat before you walk on. Perhaps we can see about getting you there safely."

Miriam looked at the man. His hands were large, rough, and dust-coated, but his eyes were kind. She felt none of the disturbing fearful excitement she had sensed in Alexander's presence, however her decisions of late had let her down so drastically that she was beginning to feel she could not even trust her own intuition. He must have seen the fear and hesitation in her eyes.

"It's ok," he continued. "I'm not going to harm you. Listen, I'll walk ten steps ahead of you and you can follow from a safe distance if you like. Before we get to my home I'll fetch Rachel, my wife. I promise you there is no danger here."

Miriam evaluated her situation. She knew she needed help and there were no other options before her other than to walk on alone down a deserted road. Despite the overwhelming anxiety that left her feeling like she wanted to run, she nodded. No further words were spoken.

Letting him walk ahead, they made their way in strange procession to an old farmhouse some five hundred yards from where she had been sitting. He turned then and spoke, having to raise his voice so she could hear him because she had stayed at a distance.

"I will go and get Rachel. You wait here."

He walked closer to the house, which was a small crumbling sandstone building with high windows and a stout wooden door. A few chickens scrabbled in the dirt in front of the house. She observed that he removed his sandals before entering and used a water jug and basin beside the door to wash his hands and face. Perhaps this was evidence that there really was a woman inside who did not want dirty feet trampling her nice clean floor.

Miriam moved into a cluster of trees a safe distance away from the house. She was ready to run at the first sign of trouble. She would walk back to Shechem alone if she had to.

From her vantage point, a few minutes later she saw young a woman appear at the door carrying a shawl. She looked this way and that as a slight frown creased her lovely face. The man joined her, and they both cast puzzled glances around the front portion of the grove next to their house.

"Where is she then?" the woman seemed to be asking.

"I don't know. Perhaps she's run off? She was quite shaken up."

"Miss? Hello?"

They called a few more times before Miriam's feet moved her out into the clearing as though they had a mind of their own. Seeing her, the couple approached cautiously, treating her like a frightened animal. Daniel stayed a respectful distance behind his wife.

"Shalom, my sister. I'm Rachel. You have already met my husband Daniel." She held out her hand. "We can help you. Would you like come into the house for some food and water? We will not harm you."

Faced with this stranger's kindness, Miriam felt her throat close up. She didn't trust it, but still tears threatened. In spite of the uncertainty, she nodded her head, and the woman gently led her towards the door.

"I'll get back to the farm then," Daniel called, and Rachel nodded.

Miriam took one last look back outside before she entered. She could see the olive trees standing in rows, their worn and twisted trunks supporting a bounty of fresh green olives. As she moved inside, she couldn't help but notice how the serenity of the orchard permeated the tiny home.

Known by the generations who had lived there as, "The Grove," the farm was a peaceful place, set on a hill with leafy views stretching into the distant mountains. According to Daniel, some of the trees were hundreds of years old.

Rachel and Daniel had not been married long, though it was clear that they loved each other dearly. They were kind and generous towards Miriam, and she ended up staying at the farm far longer than any of them had anticipated. An unforeseen detour in her journey.

Although Rachel and Daniel both made Miriam feel welcome from the very first day, initially she felt that she should not stay too long. She would eventually have to face up to the mistakes she had made when she returned to her Aunt Ellan, even if only to beg her forgiveness.

One morning as they ate a breakfast of bread and olives, Rachel spoke up, "Miriam …" She hesitated and Miriam saw her look pointedly at Daniel.

"I'm sorry to have stayed so long in your home," Miriam blurted, assuming they were going to ask her to leave. "I know I really should be going soon. I'm so grateful to you both for all you have done for me, but it's time I went home." Rachel looked slightly crest-fallen.

"Oh. Ok. We know you had planned to return to your aunt as soon as possible, and we have selfishly kept you here, but we have grown so fond of you in this short time. It's just that …"

"What?"

Daniel broke in and continued. "Would you consider staying a little longer? The harvest is coming and we could really use your help. We always employ locals and also other family members to come during harvest as it's simply too much for us to handle on our own. And since you're here and Rachel is so enjoying your company, we hoped you might stay for a while."

Miriam was silent before speaking. "You want me to stay?"

"Yes," Rachel continued. "Daniel and I have spoken about it and we both agree that it would be helpful, if it's ok with you."

Miriam couldn't help but smile and nod in agreement as she fought the tears that welled in her eyes. In the weeks that she had been there, she had grown to love The Grove. Although she had not wanted to admit it to herself, it had started to feel like home. She felt safe. If anyone was coming for her, they would surely have come here by now. She had no idea how Ellan would react to her showing up on her doorstep again, and besides, Alexander knew where her aunt lived and that she had been headed there. Gabriella's men would be keeping an eye on the house in Shechem. Perhaps it was safer to wait.

"Thank you. Thank you both. Of course, I would love to stay and help."

Rachel smiled. "Not at all. I love having you around and we make an excellent team."

"Well, now that's settled, let's get to work," Daniel smiled as he stood and walked towards the door. The women cleaned the dishes from the table and followed him outside a few minutes later. There was a new lightness in Miriam's step as she felt a burden lift from her shoulders.

When all the chores were done that day, Miriam

wandered alone through the olive grove, caressing the gnarled old trunks as she passed them. She imagined she could feel the wisdom of years running just under the surface of their bark.

What would they say if they could speak to her?

What advice would they give?

A bird's sweet song filtered down through the leaves like invisible rain, touching everything it landed upon. The blue shapes of mountains stretched across the horizon. Somewhere beyond them lay the hills of her own childhood home. Miriam decided she would try to get a messenger to her father and aunt, to apologise to them for the way she had left and to let them know she was ok.

Miriam found a compassionate confidant and authentic friend in Rachel. Over time, she told her about her mother's passing and how she could not live with her father in Sychar, so she had left and moved in with her Aunt Ellan in Shechem.

She did not dare to yet mention her first two marriages or the sham of the third. That part of the story only served to reveal her shame and vulnerability. She had shared it with Alexander, and he had used it to manipulate her. She had vowed to herself that she would not make the same mistake again.

When she got to know Rachel a little better, she opened up about Alexander and how he had tricked her. Letting her believe that he loved and wanted to marry her, weaving images of the idyllic life they would share and painting visions of raising their children in the house beside the sea. The two women cried together when Miriam shared how her dreams had been shattered when she had been forced into a life of slavery with more horror to come had she not escaped.

As she unburdened herself to Rachel, Miriam felt some of the shame lift from her shoulders. Rachel did not judge or condemn her and in the retelling of her story, it helped Miriam to let go of the pain she had been carrying for months. She mourned the loss of the Alexander she thought she knew and loved, even though he had never existed. Although this fresh grief did not compare to the cavernous grief that she had endured after losing Caleb, or the endless grief over the loss of her mother, she acknowledged that it was, nonetheless real. Once she had faced it and spoken it aloud, it seemed to hold less power over her emotions. She could not change it, but she could find a way to move forward.

Chapter XVI

A Place

Olive oil was crucial to the economy and daily living in biblical times. It was used for lighting, cooking, medicinal purposes and moisturising skin. Although black when ripe, olives used in oil production were harvested while still green. Harvesters used sticks to beat the branches, causing the fruit to fall (Isaiah 17:6; 24:13). The olives were then collected and pressed to yield oil.

A Place

Find a place where the silence
Wraps itself around your soul,
Like a blanket made of feathers
That protects against the cold.

Safe and warm and honest
Is the place where you can rest.
The silent calm will heal you
From perfectionism's constant test.

A place where you are free
From the weight of judgment's stare.
No expectations and no pressure
Will ever find you there.

A place where there is nothing
But cool air against your skin.
Just you and the horizon
With her constant beckoning.

A place where there can be no past
And no future can be seen.
All you have is the moment
As isolation leaves you clean.

Find the place where you are complete,
Just the way you are.
No striving and no sorrow
From the weight of all your scars.

A place where there is freedom
A place where you are whole,
Is the constant quest and seeking
Of every living soul.

Miriam – age 30

arvest was a flurry of activity. The Grove transformed from a quiet and peaceful sanctuary into an industry of motion and movement.

Daniel had hired his regular employees who came every year, as well as several family members who Miriam had not met before. One in particular stood out to her.

He was a quiet man. The first time she passed him with her basket of olives ready for delivery to the collection point, he looked up and smiled then quickly averted his gaze. She wondered if he was shy. Most people introduced themselves, but he did not. Yet in that fleeting moment she had seen kindness in his hazel eyes.

Then one day as she walked with Rachel through the grove, they passed him again.

"Hello John," Rachel greeted and stopped walking. Miriam hesitated beside her, surprised that they knew each other well enough for Rachel to pause.

He nodded, "Hello Rachel. Good to see you. It's been a busy season this year. A good harvest."

"Yes. The Lord has been good to us. You must come up to the house for supper. It's been a long time. It would be good to talk."

"Perhaps."

"Daniel would love to spend time with you John. Not just side by side working, but like old times."

Miriam saw what looked like pain flicker across John's face and he quickly looked away and then back again. "Perhaps I will Rachel. Thank you."

"Oh, and this is Miriam," Rachel smiled, and half turned towards her friend. "She has been staying with us for several months now. A very hard worker. Another of God's provisions and blessings I think," she laughed aloud, apparently oblivious to the discomfort that Miriam was now feeling.

John turned towards Miriam. "Nice to meet you Miriam."

Miriam nodded and Rachel again chimed in. "Well, I hope we will see you soon for supper John. Don't be a stranger."

As the women turned to leave, Miriam was sure she could feel John's eyes watching her.

Daring to ask, for now she was truly curious, she pressed Rachel for more information about this tall stranger with the gentle disposition.

"John is a cousin of Daniel's," Rachel began. "He used to live here with us at the Grove. In fact, before I married Daniel, John and Daniel ran the Grove together. John lived in the house on the other side of the hill. He owns part of this property, not that you'd know it at the moment."

"The house that sits vacant?"

"Yes, that's right. That's John's house. He lived there with his wife. It's a very sad story Miriam. After you hear it, you may think I seem a bit callous talking to him like that, pushing him to come for supper when he clearly doesn't want to. But his grief has gone on for too long now. I've spoken to Daniel about it and we both agree that he needs to start living again. It's time for him to take a hold of life again."

Miriam was surprised by Rachel's forthright words. "What happened to him?"

Rachel sighed. "He was happy. He and his wife Adina had not been married long. She was young and so full of life and spirit. Really, she was just past being a girl when they married. Perhaps about seventeen. He adored her. It was almost like he worshiped her in a way. In his eyes she could do no wrong, even though she was often climbing trees rather than taking care of her duties. But truthfully, everyone loved her. It was hard not to."

"You knew her?"

"Oh yes. We grew up together. We were friends."

"And something happened to her?" Miriam asked quietly.

"It was dreadful Miriam. I know the pain he feels as I have felt it too, although of course it is different when it's your own spouse. But I felt so sad for so long." She paused and then continued with the story. "Adina became pregnant. No one knew there was a problem with the pregnancy until it was too late. There were complications towards the end and the child had died inside but, well how could anyone know? Her baby, a little girl, was born dead. As a result, Adina then developed an infection that could not be treated. She died two days later. Oh Miriam. That poor woman died crying for her baby." Rachel hung her head as she spoke, her mind was struggling with the memories.

"John never got over the loss. Both his wife and his child suddenly gone. He changed almost instantly. He turned inwards and disappeared. First emotionally, where no one could reach him. He shut down completely. Then one day he physically disappeared. It was two years before we found out he was still alive. He had not left a word. Nothing. It devastated Daniel. Now he comes for the harvest, but only because he wants to help Daniel. He has no real investment in the property. I know it's painful for him to be here and he lives a very quiet life in town."

"How long ago did this happen Rachel?"

"It's been five or six years now. Like I said, we feel it's long enough. We were as supportive as we could be, even when he just left without warning. That could have made Daniel very angry as they ran this farm together and Daniel depended on him, but somehow, he understood."

Miriam hesitated before speaking. "What John has been through … there is no denying that loss. That kind of pain can change a person very deeply."

"It can and it has. In no way would I ever discount any of the pain he has endured. It's a long walk through the darkest of valleys. Yet he is a good man, and he is still young. He could find another wife and have a family. Time is still on his side."

"Maybe he will one day."

"Yes. Maybe he will."

John had surprised them all a few nights later when he appeared out of the blue. They had just been seated to enjoy the evening's meal when a knock interrupted them.

"John!" Rachel exclaimed in delight as she opened the door.

"Any space for one more?" he asked politely.

"Always space for you my friend," Daniel said warmly as he got up from the table and embraced his cousin.

That night around the fireplace, John had been surprisingly open about his journey. It endeared Miriam to him. As Rachel asked careful questions, he had patiently and kindly answered each one, even attempting to explain his grief. When Miram saw him struggling to find words, compassion compelled her to meet his honesty with her own.

"Sometimes our pain is too deep for words John. I have loved and lost as you have. It is a long and hard letting go, to which there can never really be an end. The pain lessens in intensity, but even years later it can sneak up on you unexpectedly. Sometimes I wonder when the last time will be that I will cry for my mother, or my husband who was killed in a tragic accident. Tears still come. Perhaps they always will."

In their honesty, the high walls of self-protection began to crumble. There was a kindling of two souls who deeply understood the valley of loss. It was the sparking of a friendship that blossomed over the coming months.

As they spoke that evening, neither John nor Miriam appeared to notice that their two companions fell silent and quietly moved away from the fireplace. Rachel busied herself with household chores. Daniel began counting his root stock and re-sorting it into baskets. Likely a task that did not need doing right then, but one that gave him a reason to allow John and Miriam space to talk.

After that night, John came regularly for supper.

It had not taken long for Miriam to fall deeply in love with John and he with her. Perhaps it had even happened without her truly realising. Friendship, trust, and authenticity sat at their core. Miriam shared with him all the misery of her past. She was able to tell him all about her first two marriages and everything that had transpired between herself and Alexander. She could not bring herself to tell him about Michael. That would forever be her personal burden of shame to bear alone.

John had asked few questions, listened compassionately, and held her close as she wept with regret. She was thankful for his love and acceptance of her, despite knowing so much about her past. Unlike Alexander, he did not use her history to exploit and control her. Instead, one evening as they walked through the olive trees after the harvest was finished and there was no fruit left on the branches, John told her that he loved her.

"Miriam, I never truly believed I would find love again. That part of my heart felt so dead and buried before I met you. Somehow, you have caused it to come back to life. I do not ever want to lose you."

He turned to look into her eyes, holding both of her hands enfolded within his own. "We are not so very young anymore. This will not be a typical arranged wedding, but would you be mine? Would you consider a man such as me for a husband?"

Miriam smiled as pure joy flooded her heart. "Of course, John. You are like a gift from God himself in my life. But …" she hesitated, and he saw it.

"But?"

She sighed. "My father. It's complicated."

John placed his hand on the side of her cheek and smiled. "We will do this the right way my darling. We will journey to your hometown and I will speak to your father."

"You would do that for me?"

"I will do anything for you Miriam."

"You know my father is likely to be very angry with me. I disappeared from his life and then from my Aunt's house. He probably thinks I'm dead." Miriam had sent messages of apology to both her Aunt Ellan and her father, but she had received no replies.

Had they received the messages? Had they refused to accept her apology? Had they cut her out of their lives and tried to erase her from memory? It was difficult to assume anything but the worst.

"Well then, he may be relieved to know that you are not only alive and well, but that you are flourishing. That you have found a man who does not need a dowry from him. A man who is self-sufficient and can take care of his daughter."

Miriam smiled. "Perhaps."

"We will travel together. Let us leave within the next few days. Harvest is over and now is the time."

It took three-days get to Sychar, and once back in her old hometown, Miriam had found it almost impossible to hold her anxiety at bay. Her father was only part of the problem. Would she have to see Nirgal? What if they bumped into him on the street? It had been a long time, but her heart remembered well how that fear tasted. And what of Michael? Miriam prayed that he would no longer even live in the town. She did not want to see him and have to pretend in front of John that she didn't know him.

Miriam was in such a state of nerves that they decided it would be best if she stayed with Mary while John went first to speak to her father. So, Miriam waited at Mary's house, pacing up and down the kitchen and driving Mary mad.

Her friend had been surprised and excited to see her again and had a thousand pressing questions that she wanted answers to, but Miram was in no frame of mind to focus. She struggled to control the intrusive thoughts that assumed the worst and brought every possible negative outcome to mind. While John's fearless nature in approaching her father made her respect him even more, she wondered how he would react when he found out what her father was like.

Mary tried to reassure her. "Miriam, I think it will be ok. It's not like John is asking for your father's seat in the temple."

Miriam giggled despite her fear. Clearly her father's reputation had not changed.

If her father did not bless their union, or even acknowledge her as his daughter, would John disappear back to his home leaving her at the mercy of her father? After all she had done, why would her father protect her? Why would he give his blessing?

Would John simply turn and walk away from her? He was under no obligation to stay. Miriam was truly terrified.

"Why don't we go for a walk into the foothills Miriam," Mary suggested. "Remember how much you used to love being out there in the wild."

"No!" she blurted out, now edged in by the fear of seeing Michael. "No, let's just stay here." She paced as Mary watched on helpless to bring any calm to her friend.

When John finally returned, he was silent for a time, sitting with his head in his hands. Miriam sat beside him and waited nervously for him to speak. Finally, he lifted his head and looked at her, taking her hand across the table.

"Miriam, it is done. I have his blessing."

"Really?"

"Yes."

"How?"

John sighed. "It's not all good news Miriam. He did give us his blessing, but I'm afraid he is very ill. Your father is dying."

"Oh! Mary didn't tell me."

"Likely because she doesn't know. His sickness has come relatively suddenly. In fact, our timing was fortunate Miriam. If we had delayed even by days, we may have been too late."

"I must go to him," Miriam said, all thoughts of past hurts evaporating like mist.

"He does not want you to see him in such a state."

"But I must go and make my peace with him," she insisted. Tears slid down her cheeks as she thought of her father passing from this world without saying a proper goodbye.

"He was emphatic. You should not come."

"John. He is my father. I must see him."

"I knew you would say this Miriam. And I told him so. I will not stop you from going to your father. Just be warned that he likely does not look like the man you knew.

I think this is why he would prefer that you stay away. He told me to take care of you. This I promised to do."

The next morning Miriam and John went together to her father's house. He lay in the bed where her mother had died. His skin was yellow, and she could see the bones in his face protruding from fragile flesh. A smell of death filled the air.

"Father?"

He turned his head and looked into the eyes of his daughter. "I knew you would come. You are stubborn, just like me."

"I'm sorry I didn't come home sooner. I could have cared for you."

"I have made peace with my God Miriam. And now I ask that we make peace. Let any hurts from the past be gone. Life is short and I have not lived it so well. Not in many ways. I was not a good father to you, but I hope you will be happy with John. You have my blessing."

She sat by his bedside for three days and could take no food. In the silence that lingered before his death, Miriam found a love for her father that she had never expected to know. A man who had tried to gain status and importance, but in the end, was just a man. Her father. A man who was once a young boy, full of all his own hopes and dreams. Somehow, life had hardened his heart and convinced him that his reputation was more important than his relationships. Here in death, he saw the truth, and she found honesty in him for the first time.

Chapter XVII

A Reason

In Israel, olive oil was used as currency, and farmers paid the owner of the olive press in oil.

The parakeet sings a melody
To wake the world with joy.
Rain gently falling
Will not halt
The praises he has to deploy.
At first light
Over shadowed trees,
He puffs out his chest and laughs.
He watches over break of day,
Like it's more precious than the last.
Then suddenly the hoopoe
And the wagtail are awake.
Rising to the challenge
Of morning melody to make.
Their song arches and then falls away,
Conducted by the light.
Voices sound
Just like pure courage,
Determined at the day's first sight.
Not one hint of complaint
Can be heard amongst the trees.
They greet the day
Like it's a miracle
That only they can see.
And I wonder…
Can I find such joy,
If I start a day with song?

With worship offered to my Maker,
Under whose wings I belong.
Do the birds understand
The power of their praise?
Do they know who holds them,
And watches over all their days?
For I have witnessed their unkept secret.
Not a morning do they waste.
Regardless of the weather,
It is sweet joy that they taste.
Their songs so unapologetic,
Ring out loud and clear,
As if trying to remind the world,
That another miracle is here.

Miriam – age 33

The curly headed boy trotted along behind her like a puppy, stopping every now and then to pick up a stick or pull a leaf from a branch. Miriam smiled and patiently waited for him to catch up. Reuben, her first born son, was almost two. She watched him with a sense of wonder, marvelling at his intense delight in the most insignificant of things. He held his latest find up to her and babbled in his baby talk as she obligingly took it from him, exclaiming the beauty of his leaf treasure – another to add to the growing collection that she dutifully carried in her hand.

"Come on, Reuben. Let's go and find Papa." She held out her hand and he reached up to take it. Together they made their slow way into the grove. John was grafting shoots from the old trees onto young stock.

"Where's Papa, Reuben? Can you see him?"

Reuben searched the trees. When he saw his father, his little legs started running, and he shouted his favourite word, Papa, over and over again.

John looked up from his work, straightened and smiled as he held his arms out to the boy, scooping him up and lifting him high into the air, before bringing him back down. He smiled at Miriam over Reuben's curly head as he snuggled into his father's shoulder. She came close, and John encircled her waist with his free arm. He nuzzled her neck, breathing in her familiar scent. It reminded him of honey and cinnamon and fresh bread.

"We brought you some food," Miriam offered as she held out the bundle.

"Wonderful. I could do with a rest."

They sat down in a clearing of lush grass. Miriam never tired of the serenity of the grove. Reuben waddled over and plonked himself down in her lap. She stroked his dark hair until he snuggled down with a chubby thumb in his mouth and fell fast asleep. Sitting in these beautiful surroundings with her little family, Miriam felt completely content and happy.

They feasted on olives and fresh bread dipped in oil that had been seasoned with salt. John took a long drink of fresh water from the wine skin Miriam had brought. Then he leaned over and gently placed his hand on her swollen belly. They exchanged a knowing smile over the head of little Reuben.

"Not long now," Miriam whispered. Caught up in the mystery of the second child that was growing inside her, she wondered whether it would be a boy or a girl this time? What would this child be like? Would it look like John, as Rueben did, or would it take after her?

Soon, the wait would be over, and she would know. She both dreaded and eagerly longed for the day this baby would come into the world.

Miriam looked over at John and realised that his thoughts mirrored her own. She noticed the deep concern that momentarily darkened his features and knew he had good reason to fear for her safety and the child's. Strong, self-sufficient and competent, John had been completely lost and terrified when she went into labour with Rueben. His own past trauma could not be held at bay and the fear overwhelmed him. But Rachel had been there and she was an excellent midwife. Rachel would be there for this next birth too.

"It will be okay," Miriam squeezed his hand reassuringly.

"I pray so." She nodded, knowing that his faith was strong and true. They were in God's hands.

They sat in silence for a long time, relishing the sound of their son's gentle snores as the wind rustled a lullaby in the leaves above them. Miriam loved the way the golden olive leaves glowed in the dappled light.

"How is the grafting going?"

"Good I think, but only time will tell. I have some potential shoots from the old trees my great grandfather planted. If they take, it would be like giving them the chance to begin afresh. The old become new. Isn't that an amazing thought? Perhaps one day, Reuben will tell his grandchildren how his father grafted the trees his own children play under."

Miriam smiled. "I hope so."

The Grove had become her sanctuary. It always reminded her of the story about how God had fed the Israelites in the wilderness. They had called the food that fell from heaven, 'mana', which meant 'what is it?' They had not initially understood the gift God had provided. In the same way, she had not recognised the Grove as her own mana. She had not dared to believe that it was the answer to her prayers. Yet, in this place, God had provided exactly what she needed. She had found John, and together they had built the life she had once only dreamed of.

Rachel supported Miriam's shoulders as the next contraction took hold. The pain was unbearable, and after hours of labour, Miram felt weak, her body trembling uncontrollably between contractions. Beads of sweat formed on her brow, Rachel wiped them away before they could run into her eyes.

"I don't think I can go on much longer," Miriam told her through gritted teeth.

"You have no choice Miriam." Rachel's voice was firm, but also calm and reassuring. "Now, listen to me."

"I can't. I can't." Miriam surrendered to panic. Rachel put her hands around Miriam's face and gently turned her head so she could look directly into her eyes.

"Listen to me. This is the transition where that feeling of panic is normal. That means it's almost over Miriam. You're almost done. You can do this. When the next contraction comes, I want you to push until I tell you to stop. Okay?" Rachel had reposited herself so she was ready.

Fighting the overwhelm, Miriam nodded and let

out a deep groan as the contraction enveloped her like an avalanche. Exhausted as she was, she knew that she had to climb the mountain again.

"Okay Miriam, now push. That's it. Good."
Miriam's body heaved. She tried to distract herself from the pain with thoughts of running through the foothills above Sychar. She saw the yellow desert grass beneath her bare feet. Saw her toes wriggling in the river. She heard her mother's voice calling her name in that familiar singsong tone, "Miriam, Miriam."

"Miriam, I said stop pushing. Listen to me."
Rachel's voice snapped her back to reality. She looked at her friend as the contraction subsided once more.

"The next one will come quickly Miriam. You did well. I want you to push again."

"I can't, I can't," her irrational mind whirled in panic.

"Once more. With the next contraction your baby should be here."

As the pain hit her, Miriam pushed with all her might, then she felt a rush of relief as her body let go of the life it had been holding secret all these months. She sank back as Rachel lifted the small wet bundle and placed the baby onto Miriam's chest.

Miriam was in awe, oblivious now to Rachel still working to cut the umbilical cord and care for the details that suddenly seemed irrelevant to Miriam.

"It's a girl," Miriam whispered with a joyful sign.

"Thank you Lord."

The little girl gave a gentle cry and Miriam cradled her close, her own body giving warmth to this new life.

Once she was cleaned up, Rachel helped her to settle on a pile of cushions in a corner of the room. Sleep suddenly loomed over her, silent and beckoning, but she railed against it, wanting only to hold her baby.

"Miriam." She opened her eyes and realised that she must have drifted off to sleep. Rachel was holding a bundle wrapped in a white linen cloth. She gently passed the baby to her mother. "She's beautiful," said Rachel.

Miriam smiled and cried as she looked down at her baby. Tiny dark curls peeped out of her swaddling. Just like mine, Miriam thought. The baby's dark eyes peered up at Miriam. She was indeed beautiful. Perfect. Miriam unwrapped the linen just a little to get a clearer look at the exquisite little creature she could call her own. Her daughter.

"Should I go and tell John?" asked Rachel. Miriam nodded.

Within minutes he was standing beside her, smiling and stroking her damp hair as a tear slid down his cheeks.

"Well done, my darling. She is beautiful. We shall call her Naomi."

"Naomi," Miriam whispered.

"Yes. Naomi, meaning beautiful." John smiled and nodded, stroking the baby's cheek with his large finger. "Just like her mother."

Chapter XVIII

The War Is Mine

The Torah is the Samaritan religion's sacred text. (It is also now known as the first five books of the Old Testament, but for the Samaritan people it stands alone.) Within the text of the Torah, women were often considered part of a man's possessions, along with his children, slaves, and livestock. However, the relationship was mutually beneficial as a man held a responsibility to provide for his wife and children. (Exodus 20:17; Deuteronomy 5:21)

Sometimes there are just no words
And the song, it just won't play,
So, in the silence we must wait
To listen close for what You say.

You teach us patience in the testing
And obedience through the pain.
You do not waste a single tear
As they gently wash the heart stains.
You see every hidden wound.
Every silent cry you hear.
You hold close every call for help
And carry every tear.

And as You draw us into battle
Right up to the front line,
That's when You move us to the side
And say, "This war is mine."

Miriam – age 35

Rueben and Naomi grew like little flowers in the spring – fearless and determined. They adored one another and Reuben took great pride in helping Miriam care for "his baby". Although only a toddler, he possessed the heart of a guardian – just like his father.

The Grove was their home and they lived comfortably and happily amongst the olive trees. Miriam found that she had no desire to ever leave. Rachel had a daughter of her own now and together the women managed the households while John and Daniel became partners once again in the running of the farm. Between the four of them, a deep and steadfast friendship had blossomed.

Although the biggest profits came from selling their olives to oil producers, Rachel went to the local markets each week with fresh and pickled olives, pastes and condiments. Miriam sold the same produce at a small road-side stall they had set up at the farm gate.

It was there that she stood in her usual position by the stall one afternoon, when she found herself suddenly confronted by her past.

Reuban played with pebbles and a stick nearby, creating shapes and imaginary worlds in his mind. Naomi was fast asleep in a pouch on Miram's back. Although she was a two year old, it was still her favourite place to sleep. Strapped to her mother.

It was drawing towards the end of a hot summer's day, and there were few travellers on the road. Miriam unhooked a veil from her headscarf and smiled down at her son as she began to pack up. She was bent double, packing jars of preserved olives into their cart, when she sensed a customer waiting.

Forgetting to secure her veil, she stood up and turned to face the tall, oddly-familiar figure. The smile froze on her face and was quickly replaced by abject terror as she recognised the man on the other side of the table. Alexander!

Their eyes locked in a moment of instant recognition and shock. Neither spoke. A thousand thoughts flashed through her mind. She fought the compulsion to grab a hold of Reuben and run back into the grove, but knew she would never be able to outpace him, should he follow. Not with Reuben beside her and Naomi strapped to her back.

He smiled slowly and when he did finally speak, it was in a strange and deliberate manner that unnerved her even further.

"Well ... Hello Miriam. What a lovely surprise to find you here."

Pinned by his intense gaze and snakelike smile, she could not move. How had she never before noticed the evil that lived in that smile?

"What's wrong with you my dear? You look so worried. Aren't you happy to see me?" He looked around and up over his head in mock confusion.

"Please leave." It sounded feeble even to her own ears, but it was all she could manage.

"Leave?" Alexander managed to look offended. "That's a very rude way to speak to a customer. They really should have taught you better manners here, but as I recall," he paused for effect, "you were never good at listening to instructions."

"I want you to leave. Now." She said, regaining some composure. She had to pull it together and protect her children.

"I would like a pot of green olives, please?" She only stared at him wondering how and why he would he keep up this charade. When she didn't move, he knelt and spoke directly to Reuben. "Excuse me, young man, I'd like some olives plea—" Miriam pulled Reuban behind her back, shielding him from Alexander's sight.

"Do not speak to him."

"Is this the way you treat the man who saved your life?"

Miriam ignored him. She could stand it no longer. Giving in to the urge to flee, she swept a protesting Reuben up in her arms and half walked, half ran up the hill back into the safety of the Grove.

"Miriam, oh come on Miriam, I just want some olives," he shouted. Initially she thought he would not follow, but as she turned her head to check, she saw him coming.

"No, no, no," she whispered under her breath as she tried to move faster. Reuban stopped protesting and began crying as he sensed the unusual fear in his mother.

She could hear Alexander getting closer, calling her name, instructing her to turn around and assuring her that he just wanted to talk. When his pressure did not work, he began hurling insults at her.

Both children were wailing now. Miriam felt her heart might burst with fear and anger. Pressing Reuben's head tightly to her breast, she kept going as fast as she could. She had almost made it to the top of the hill when she felt her strength failing. Her arms and legs ached. Her breath came in ragged gasps. Just when she thought Alexander would finally catch them, she ran blindly into John's broad chest. He had heard the commotion and come over at a run.

He took her into his arms with Reuben sandwiched between their bodies and held her tight. Over her head, he saw Alexander just a few paces away. "What's going on?" John asked.

"It's him." Miriam gasped. John knew immediately what she meant and she saw a strange expression cross John's face. It was a look she had never seen before. Without taking his eyes off Alexander, who had stopped dead in his tracks at the sight of John, in a whispered voice he instructed, "Take the children home. Send Daniel."

"John?" Miriam looked from John to Alexander and back again.

"Go."

Miram wanted to protest, but Reuben and Naomi began wailing again, and she knew she had no choice. She had to bring her children to safety. She ran to Rachel's farmhouse as fast as her legs could carry her.

Miriam burst into the house, and seeing Rachel, she cried out, "Where's Daniel?"

"Miriam? What's wrong?"

"It's Alexander." She was puffing so much it was difficult to speak. "He came to the stall. He recognised me. I ran. John came and told me to send Daniel. Where is he?" Miriam shouted in her terror.

"He's still out in the groves, but he should be home soon." Rachel had to raise her voice also to be heard over the noise of the crying children. Her own baby, Ruth, had joined in from the next room.

"I must go and find him." Miriam headed for the door, but Rachel stopped her.

"Wait, you take care of the children. Let me find Daniel." Lifting a distressed Reuben out of her arms, Rachel helped Miriam to free Naomi from the leather pouch. "Now, sit down and give Naomi a feed. I'll get Reuben and Ruth settled then I'll find Daniel. You must stay here Miriam."

Miriam didn't want to sit down and feed Naomi while John might be in danger, but she knew Rachel was right. There was nothing she could do now. Finally, Rachel headed to the door and all Miriam could do was pray Daniel would not be far away.

"Miriam, bolt the door behind me," Rachel called as she left.

Miriam struggled to settle herself as fear like an old familiar friend crept into her bones. She placed Reuben on a chair giving him a handful of dates to chew on. Gradually, Ruth had fallen back to sleep and her children's wails subsided into hiccups. Naomi had settled too and was suckling contentedly at Miriam's breast.

Miriam wiped a tear from her cheek. She tried desperately to be calm and not imagine the worst, but a terrible sick feeling would not leave her. It sat like a beast that was mocking her to the core.

Finally, after what felt like an eternity, there was a knock at the door.

"Open the door Miriam. It's me Rachel."

Chapter XIX

Drops Of Rain

Matthew 5:4

Blessed are those who mourn, for they will be comforted.

Drops Of Rain

Drops of rain confound
The hardness of the soul
As tender mercy falls
And lands gentle as the snow.

Washing away foundations
Built up like valley walls.
Washing away everything
You thought could never fall.

Individual bursts of cold
Fill eyelids once so dry.
Rainfall sweet and tender
As teardrops fall from sky.

Let it just come gentle
Before the river flows.
A little burst in the dam wall
To ease the pressure on the soul.

They say it is important.
They say it must begin.
They say a heart in hiding
Can only heal from deep within.

And the rain, it is a cleansing
Like the tears as they begin to fall,
Washing every memory
At every hard recall.

Standing in the downpour
Watching life move by,
Healing seeps in slowly here
With every tear we cry.

Miriam – age 35

John lay on his sleeping mat as he had for the last several weeks, his body wracked with fever. Bereft and afraid, Miriam stroked his brow.

Small fragments of prayers escaped her lips, though her eyes rarely left his face, seeking warmth and life beneath his pale skin. Her heart felt like it might shatter into a billion pieces.

Nights and days blurred, and time ceased to hold any meaning for her as she waited impatiently for her husband to wake up.

Rachel urged her to eat, if not for her sake, then for Naomi who was still nursing, but Miriam barely touched her food.

John was fighting. Miriam was sure of that. Even though she could not see the battle he was engaged in, she knew that he would find a way back to her. She imagined that he was trapped in a dark maze and was searching for a way out.

Could he hear her as she called to him?

Could he feel her hands on his face?

Could he see some spark of light that would lead him back into her waiting arms?

John had been like this, trapped between this world and the next since the day that Alexander had come and turned their lives upside down.

By the time Daniel arrived at the place where Miriam had left the two men, Alexander was nowhere to be found, and John was lying on the ground. His scull had been dashed against a rock and a steady flow of blood pooled beneath his head.

He was barely breathing when Daniel had carried him home. The sight of her lifeless husband was shocking and devastating. By the second week, the fever had taken hold of him. All they could do was keep him as comfortable as possible and pray. Pray for a miracle.

Miriam wished she had stayed beside John. She wished Daniel had got to them sooner. She railed against the injustice of it all. She knew there was no point in driving herself mad with regret, but still dark thoughts taunted her as she kept vigil beside the man she loved.

John had so much life ahead of him. She dreaded having to live without him by her side.

Would her dreams always be smashed apart like avalanches of rock cascading down the sides of a steep canyon? Why? Oh why? There were no answers.

On occasion, her thoughts also turned to Alexander, and though she knew in her heart that she would likely never see him again, she dreamed of revenge.

The dreadful wound at the base of John's skull now gave off a pungent odour when she removed the bandage. Streams of yellow and green puss oozed out between the black scabs of blood. The sight and stench, broke Miriam's heart, and at the same time, made her wretch.

A gasp made Miriam turn from her work to see Rachel standing behind her. She had brought Naomi to her for a feed.

"Oh Miriam." In those two simple words, Rachel managed to convey all the horror and heartache Miriam felt. She set the little girl down gently on a cushion.

"Miriam, let me help you."

"No Rachel. I'll do it." Miriam bent over her husband, attempting to wipe away the puss with a piece of sponge soaked in vinegar. Rachel knelt beside her. She looked over at John and could see how lifeless and emaciated he had become in a few short weeks. His breath was shallow and raspy now. She put her hand on Miriam's forearm.

"Has he taken any water?"

"No."

"Has he stirred at all?"

"No."

"Oh, my friend."

"Please don't say it, Rachel. There's still hope. Miracles can happen."

Rachel bowed her head and closed her eyes. She began to pray under her breath. As she did so, John's breathing altered, becoming ragged and uneven. Miriam recognised the death rattle. She had heard it when her mother took her last breaths. The hope she had held onto so tightly, was slipping through her fingers.

Rachel looked at her in fear. Their eyes met and a strange calmness, that Miriam had never known before in the face of death, began to wash over her. An acceptance that she did not expect to ever feel. She found words from somewhere deep within. She leaned in close and put her head gently onto John's chest.

"John, my darling," she said. "I love you so very much. I'm here. I'm right here by your side. You're not alone."

Rachel stood and picked up Naomi who was beginning to fuss. She soothed the baby in the far corner of the room, gazing through the window at the olive trees, tears streaming silently down her cheeks.

"Thank you, John," said Miriam. "Thank you for giving me so much and letting me find love in your arms. You mean everything to me. I love you. And I'm so sorry that this has happened. Oh, my darling, I love you. "

She stroked his matted hair, brushing it off his sweat-drenched forehead. "It's okay my darling. You are so strong, John, but you can stop fighting now. I want you to stay with me forever, but if you need to go, it's okay. I understand. I will take care of our children and raise them in a way that will make you proud."

Had he heard her? She could not be sure, but for a fleeting moment, she thought she saw a flicker behind his closed eyes. A silent acknowledgment. Then his breathing stopped altogether.

It was over.

Rachel came to sit beside her. The two women knelt together in a sisterly embrace with little Naomi between them. And they wept.

Chapter XX

Ashes

*Shomron, the **Hebrew** translation of Samaria, literally means watch mountain or watch tower.*

Ashes

When all you see are ashes
And all your efforts turn to dust,
Do not be discouraged,
For God makes oceans from that stuff.

He makes flowing fertile valleys
Out of barren land.
He makes mountains out of deserts
And forests out of sand.

He makes flowers bloom up through the ground.
He fills the clouds with rain.
He has a way of making what is hopeless
Breathe new life again.

He makes galaxies from stardust
And in case you haven't heard,
The entirety of creation
Was birthed upon His word.

It never gets too messy
And it never gets too hard,
For the God at work within your chaos
Is the One who formed the stars.

So when all you see is ash and dust
And you're ready to give in,
Smile instead - because you know,
This is exactly where He will begin.

Miriam – age 36

The days after John's passing had moved by slowly. Pain filled the spaces she walked within, and after a time, it morphed into a deep numbness that settled over her like a heavy wet blanket. Miriam retreated into a shell.

Her withdrawal frightened Rachel, who tried constantly to help her re-engage with life. For Rachel, it was like living a nightmare all over again. John had disappeared from them when he lost his first wife. Now her dear friend and sister Miriam seemed to have fallen into the same bottomless canyon. Rachel did all she could. She insisted that she needed help at the markets and dragged Miriam along, but it proved disastrous. Miriam could not focus, and instead jumped at random sounds and strangers. She sat watching for Alexander's face, as if he might walk around a corner at any moment. Rachel had feared what Miriam would do, had he indeed appeared. Thankfully he did not, but Rachel did not continue insisting that Miriam take these outings to the market. Instead, she tried to distract Miriam every evening, with stories about the farm. Miriam could barely listen. Rachel could not seem to find the key to help her emerge from behind the bolted door of her grief and sorrow.

In that first year, there were many times when Miriam touched the depths of a despair so deep that she no longer wanted to live. Even though she was no stranger to loss, she had not experienced this intensity of grief before.

A hopelessness so all-consuming that she felt that her life was not worth living. She just wanted the pain to stop and even began fantasising about how she could end it all and make it look like an accident. A fall from a cliff on a rainy day when the rocks were slippery. An unexplained illness. Her mind often took her absently into dark places, like it was attempting to find a way to retreat from the grief. It was only her sense of love and responsibility towards her children that kept her placing one foot in front of the other day after day. She had promised John that she would raise them well. Without them, she felt like there was no longer any future and life seemed devoid of all meaning. The colour drained from all aspects of life, leaving only grey.

The Grove, once her sanctuary, had begun to feel suffocating. She no longer walked among the trees, instead staying inside or close to the house. The rows and rows of olive trees reminded her too much of John's strength and kindness. Like the trees in the grove, he had sheltered and nourished her. Now she was once again alone.

The Grove had also begun changing. Daniel was battling his own grief while trying to keep the farm running, and at times it felt like a losing battle. He desperately needed more help and had begun employing passing travellers. They were given food and lodging in exchange for several days' work. It was not a substitute for John's managerial skills, but it helped hold things at bay for a season.

One afternoon Miriam sat on the stoop outside the

house as she absently watched Reuban and Naomi play in the grass. Although it was a beautiful day, with sunlight shining on the last of the summer's grasses that composed a colourful array of tiny blooming flowers, she did not see any joy in it. Her mind was lost in the fog of despair, but she tried hard to be physically present for the children.

Several women whom she did not recognise, stood a few meters away picking olives and throwing them into baskets. They chatted casually as they worked, and Miriam began to pick up on snatches of their conversation.

"So Sychar?"

"Yes. In a few days we will begin."

"I hear that the market in the town is thriving these days."

"We need to get there before the weather turns."

"I'll speak to Ezra. I know he is happy to stay here, but we must push forward."

"Yes, I agree. Speak to him tonight."

"Excuse me?" Miriam approached the women with little forethought. "I heard you speaking about Sychar. Are you going there?"

The women looked at her and smiled. "Yes. You know it? We are taking our wears there from the women in our town. To sell in the markets."

"It's always good to have a fresh audience," laughed the other woman.

"What are you selling?" Miriam enquired.

"Scarves. Tunics. Hand made by a group of us at

home in Joppa. We're looking for new markets to grow our business."

"Oh. That sounds good," Miriam tried to show genuine interest.

"We will show you later if you like?"

Miriam nodded, "Thank you. I'd like that." She hesitated before speaking again. "Sychar is my hometown. I am thinking of returning there myself. Do you think I could join your group and travel with you? I can pay my own way, and when we get to Sychar, I will introduce you to some of the women there who will help you organise a space at the markets."

The women looked at each other in surprise before the older of the two spoke. "I will talk to my husband Ezra, but I think that should be no problem."

And so it was that a year after John's passing, Miriam, Reuben and Naomi joined the group of merchants and made the long trip back to Sychar, to her childhood home.

As a mature mother of two, no longer bearing the heavy weight of shame and fear, Miriam hoped Sychar might offer her a fresh start. A place where her children could find community in a town rather than isolated on a farm. She could live in the house that her father had left to her and deep down she hoped for connection with the friends she had grown up with.

But something else was waiting for her in Sychar too. Something she had closed the door on a long time ago.

Returning to Sychar was bittersweet in so many ways. Both her mother and father were no longer there, and she slipped into town unnoticed. The house was as she had left it at her father's passing. She ushered the children inside and set to work lighting some lanterns.

"I want to go home." Reuban stated again. She had heard those words many times in the days since they had left the Grove, and they stung her heart like little knives.

Was she doing the right thing?

How could she take her children away from the only home they had ever known?

Miriam sat down next to Reuban and put her arm around him. "I know son. I'll tell you what, we will stay here for a bit and if we really don't like it, we can go home ok?"

"But why mama? Why do we have to stay here? I want Aunty Rachel. I want to go back home."

"Well, there are lots of other boys and girls here about your age and Sychar is a nice town. You might make some good friends."

"I don't want friends," he cried. "I want Aunty Rachel and Uncle Daniel. I want to go home."

Miriam sighed and stood up, feeling suddenly frustrated by Reuban's unwillingness to listen. He was only young, but already stubborn when he didn't get his own way.

"I'll make us some nice supper. Go and set your bag next to the bed in that room."

Reuban did not answer or move but she chose to leave the battle for another time. She knew he was scared and didn't understand why they had to leave the Grove. In the last year he had lost his father and now she was asking him to also say goodbye to his home. It all just felt impossibly hard in that moment, and she could not think beyond it. Just get them fed and to sleep. Tomorrow is a new day.

Despite a first restless night, she rose early in the morning and got the children ready. They needed fresh water and something in her was looking forward to the familiar walk to the well. She would surprise her friends there with their return.

The worn path at the edge of town at sunrise had not changed with the passage of time. Miriam wondered if indeed it had somehow been suspended, like it was waiting for her to return. A crazy thought, but the overwhelming feeling of the familiar enveloped her and suddenly her grief felt a little less tangible. A little further away from her present reality. The rays of sunlight, golden on the grasslands, just as they had always been at daybreak. The quiet steps of other women as they raced the emerging sun.

It was a feeling of being a part of a path that was trodden by the generations before her, and the ones still to come. She was but a link in the chain. A small piece of a bigger picture.

"Miriam?" Helen was already at the well when they arrived, and she stopped drawing water at the surprise of seeing her old friend. A few other familiar faces were also there, and Miram smiled and nodded a greeting as she spoke.

"Hello Helen."

"You're here?" she stated the obvious in a question.

"Yes, I'm here. These are my children Helen. This is Reuban and this is Naomi."

"Oh Miriam, they're lovely. But … why are you here?"

"My husband passed. I needed to come home." It was as concise an explanation as she could give, that told Helen all she needed to know. Her friend stepped forward to embrace her, and Miriam felt the tears running down her cheeks.

"Welcome home sister," Helen whispered. "Tonight, you and the children must come for supper."

Miriam nodded and smiled as hope sparked bright in her chest.

In the months following their return, Miriam and the children settled. Reuban soon made friends with the other children his age and his incessant asking to go home gradually lessoned. He would often leave the house early to go and find his friends while she walked to the well with Naomi.

Miriam found a rhythm in the days that helped her focus. There was always work to be done. Keeping her hands busy kept her mind from too much thinking, and her heart from too much grief. Slowly it began to ebb. The edges of it less sharp and raw. She found herself smiling, and even laughing with her own community. There was strength in their bond. So much that didn't need to be spoken because of their shared history. They knew each other in a way that only sisters can.

Late one evening, Miriam heard a knock at the door. She stopped kneading the bread for the morning meal to listen. The knock came again.

Strange. I wonder who is here at this time?

She approached the door. "Who is it?"

"Miriam? It's me, Michael."

Shock flooded Miriam. She had not seen Michael since her return and had not asked anyone about him. Words felt like they stuck in her throat.

"Michael? What are you doing here?" Her heart beat a drum against her ribs as she opened the door a crack. His familiar eyes shone in the dim light. His skin had been a little weathered by the years, but he was the same broad shouldered, handsome man she remembered.

"What are you doing here?" she repeated.

"Nice to see you too." He smiled. "Can I come in?"

"No! Absolutely not. Don't you know what that would mean for me if you were caught in my house? Besides my children are asleep and …"

"I just want to talk."

"You can't come in. It's after dark."

"Then you come out. We can stand in full view of everyone so no one can accuse you of anything."

"Michael!"

He stepped away to a communal sitting area often used in the daytime by the neighbours. "I'll sit here. You can sit far on the other side."

He looked too big for the small seat, as if his frame wasn't made to rest on things made by hand. Then she noticed the nervousness in his eyes and felt a wave of compassion towards him.

Miriam emerged and sat on a stool in the furthest corner of the seated area as far from him as possible.

"This is awkward," he stated. She stared at him with raised eyebrows and unspoken questions.

"You never said goodbye," he said. She had no words and no excuse to give him. A silence hung between them. When he continued, she sensed no accusation or unkindness, only genuine concern and the deep pain that she had caused. "I heard the news of your marriage."

Miriam remained mute.

What could she tell him? She had been too cowardly to face him.

"I loved you, Miriam."

Miriam sensed the danger and wanted to end the conversation. Even though they were not behind closed doors, if anyone overheard him speaking so openly to her she would be accused, flogged, or worse. She had her children to think of now.

Did Michael not understand the risk?

"Please stop. Don't say such things," she whispered.

"Our love was true."

"It was impossible."

"But why marry Nirgal, of all people? Everyone knew he was a bully." His voice rose in frustration.

"Be quiet!" Miriam looked desperately around, but it did appear as though they were alone.

"Sorry," he looked contrite. "I'm just trying to understand."

"I can't speak to you here. I'm going inside. Please don't come here again. If you have things to say to me, well I'm just not sure how that will work. Maybe we can talk with … no … I don't know."

"Wait. Just wait, before you go. I don't need answers to the past. I just wanted to see you, and maybe see if there is a chance for us."

"I have children Michael. They are my priority now."

Miriam turned towards her front door a few steps away and opened the door to go inside.

"Miriam." He was right behind her. She could almost feel his warmth.

Turning, Miriam blocked the doorway and stood her ground.

"You must go. This is not the way. If you respect me

at all you will leave now."

Michael sighed heavily. "I see. Very well. Goodbye for now Miriam."

She watched him walk away with a feeling of dread creeping into her heart. Michael pushing his way back into her life could only mean trouble and she was too tired for trouble. Miriam sensed an urgency to protect herself and her children from whatever intensions towards her he might have.

Chapter XXI

Byway

Matthew 1:1-17

The book of the genealogy of Jesus Christ,

the son of David, the son of Abraham.

Abraham was the father of Isaac,

and Isaac the father of Jacob,

and Jacob the father of Judah and his brothers,

and Judah the father of Perez and Zerah by Tamar,

and Perez the father of Hezron,

and Hezron the father of Ram,

and Ram the father of Amminadab,

and Amminadab the father of Nahshon,

and Nahshon the father of Salmon,

and Salmon the father of Boaz by Rahab,

and Boaz the father of Obed by Ruth,

and Obed the father of Jesse,

and Jesse the father of David the king.

And David was the father of Solomon by the wife of Uriah,

and Solomon the father of Rehoboam,

and Rehoboam the father of Abijah,

and Abijah the father of Asaph,

and Asaph the father of Jehoshaphat,

and Jehoshaphat the father of Joram,

and Joram the father of Uzziah,

and Uzziah the father of Jotham,

and Jotham the father of Ahaz,

and Ahaz the father of Hezekiah,

and Hezekiah the father of Manasseh,

and Manasseh the father of Amos,

and Amos the father of Josiah,

and Josiah the father of Jechoniah and his brothers,

at the time of the deportation to Babylon.

And after the deportation to Babylon:

Jechoniah was the father of Shealtiel,

and Shealtiel the father of Zerubbabel,

and Zerubbabel the father of Abiud,

and Abiud the father of Eliakim,

and Eliakim the father of Azor,

and Azor the father of Zadok,

and Zadok the father of Achim,

and Achim the father of Eliud,

and Eliud the father of Eleazar,

and Eleazar the father of Matthan,

and Matthan the father of Jacob,

and Jacob the father of Joseph the husband of Mary,

of whom Jesus was born, who is called Christ.

So all the generations from Abraham to David were fourteen generations, and from David to the deportation to Babylon fourteen generations, and from the deportation to Babylon to the Christ, fourteen generations.

Byway

I took the long road home,
And lingered down the dusty road,
Kicked stones along the byway
And watched the life unfold.

A small butterfly flew past
My tainted point of view.
Its life lived free upon the wind,
With wings spread wide
It flew.

It seemed to be beckoning,
Like it knew some secret
I should know too.
Some fundamental key I'd missed,
That might alter all I do.

It stopped me still as if to say,
I must redeem the time,
For life cannot be held onto
As if it were all mine.

The gift is always passing,
Always running fast away.
Like a stream that travels constant
From hidden spring to unseen grave.

As you watch – it falls.
As you pause – it moves.
Unravelling the constant thread
Of all the life we lose.

So, I spread my wings out wide,
Just to see what might unfold.
I let go of all agenda
And pressing stories I'd been sold.

I gave myself permission
To breathe out and let the pressure go,
And found life on the dusty byway,
As I made my slow way home.

Miriam – age 38

No life is a predictable journey from beginning to end. It is neither prescribed nor possible to foresee where one starts and will end up. Miriam had learned this in many ways. Despite all the religious rules and ideologies of Samaritan culture that had governed most aspects of her life from the day she was born, there had often been an undercurrent that seemed to drag her in a different direction. The regrets she carried waged war with her need for peace, and sometimes it felt like she was in a constant internal battle that no one else could see. Yet she was older and wiser now, and at this time, at this junction, she was determined to make sensible choices for the sake of her children. Choices that were based on logic and not her heart's leadings.

Michael was once the man she had dreamed of, but now he scared her. His advances made her feel vulnerable, like a caged bird that had no defence. He reappeared on her doorstep a number of times and offered her support and companionship, yet she knew they could not risk pursuing the relationship this time. Her duty to her children would not permit her to behave in the carefree way she once had, and this was something Michael seemed incapable of understanding. His life had not altered as hers had. He had never married and continued to remain as carefree as his flocks high up in the hills. A life full of daydreams and far from the restraints of duty.

Miriam was caught between her genuine affection

for Michael, and her need to follow the social rules. In so doing, she had no choice but to find a husband from her own social class. Someone who would provide for her children and give them the best chance at a good future. She reasoned that it might also be a way to encourage Michael to leave her alone.

Her third-cousin Uri was a man who had been making inquiries about her. Miriam had heard this gossip from her friends, who heard it from their husbands, who presumably heard it from Uri himself. So, Miriam was not overly surprised when Uri arrived at the door together with her great uncle, to make his intentions clear.

"We are here to help your situation," her uncle began as they sat down around her sparce kitchen table. Her uncle Eli was the younger brother to Miriam's father, and not someone she had ever known well. As a young girl, it was simply not possible or considered appropriate for her to mix freely with the male members of her family. Yet here he was now sitting at her kitchen table, with her distant cousin Uri. Miriam mused that it was possibly the first time in her life that she had held a conversation with either of these men. Uri was perhaps twenty years older than her. His children were grown, and his wife had passed a year earlier.

"Miriam." He spoke with formality. "You are a single woman living again in Sychar. As you know, this is simply not an acceptable situation for you and your children to be in. Your father would be rolling over in his grave if he knew that you were here in his house and living all alone with two children. He left the house to you, yes, but so that you might return with your husband one day. We could now send you away again, back to where your former husband lived, as that is where you belong and therefore need to stay. However, Uri has presented our counsel with another option for us to consider. The men in your family have agreed, that you and Uri would make an acceptable match, and in so doing, you will secure your children's future here in Sychar."

Miriam was momentarily lost for words. She wanted to argue but knew there was simply no point. Her uncle was not a man of idle threat. If she did not marry an acceptable man, she was going to be sent back.

Suddenly Uri spoke, breaking the silence. "Miriam, I will be honest. I am getting older. My beloved wife passed and I am lonely and in need of a wife to help me in everyday life. I don't ask much in return for the security I can provide for you and your children."

"Thank you," Miriam found her voice. "Your offer is very kind."

"I have a big house and you may come there. This house you may keep to do with as you please, should you agree."

"May I ask, without being presumptuous, what you require?" Was the question too forthright? Miriam squirmed in her chair as the men looked at one another. Again, it was Uri who broke the uncomfortable silence.

"As I said my dear, I need a companion and help. That is all. I do not want a servant. I want a wife. You and your children will be provided for."

Her uncle chimed in. "Miriam, here is the situation. Uri makes you a very generous offer. If you refuse, then we will ask for the sake of the community, that you return to your former husband's family, for this is where you belong."

"It is a generous offer," Miriam agreed. "Uri, I thank you for the kindness you have shown. I … I will accept your offer."

Finally, Uri and her uncle smiled. "A good decision Miriam," her uncle exclaimed. "Your father would be proud."

The wedding was an uneventful affair. To Miriam's immense relief, Uri showed little interest in her other than as a companion. He did his duty to consummate the marriage and thereafter seldom invited her to share his bed. She was free to sleep in her children's room throughout the night so long as she would rise early to make him a morning meal.

Though Uri was an important man in the town's business and religious sectors, he was also a kind man, who was willing to help raise her children. Miriam played the role of the dutiful wife and found the arrangement quite palatable. In fact, she found herself becoming quite fond of him as the months passed.

She did not see Michael for many months. Miriam reasoned that he had presumably discovered she was remarried and had moved away from her father's house. Then one night after Uri and the children were asleep, there was a knock at the front door. A servant answered. Then came to call her from one of the servants.

"Sorry Mam, but there is a messenger at the door. He insists on speaking to you in person."

"Thank you." Miriam hurried to the door with an aching certainty in her belly that she knew who this stranger would be.

"What are you doing here?" she demanded.

"I'm in torment, Miriam."

She stood with her arms folded across her chest, staring at him. Fighting her desire to reach out and embrace him.

"Don't you see? It has to be this way, Michael. I need a father for my children more than I need a lover in my bed," she hissed. Stricken by her harsh words, he took a step backwards. Steeling herself, Miriam was about to say more when Reuben's frightened voice came from inside the house.

"Mummy. Mummy." This startled Miriam into action.

"You have to go. You can't be here. Go away and never return."

Without waiting for a reply, she closed the door and went over to where her son stood. She bent over him as he rubbed his eyes with his fists. "I had a bad dream. A bad man was chasing me. And I was running, but I couldn't run fast enough. I'm scared Mummy." Miriam hugged him tight. She could feel his little heart still beating fast.

"It's okay, my darling," she soothed. "I'm here. It was just a dream."

"But it was so real, Mummy."

"I know darling. I know. It's not real though. It's just pretend." She put him back down and pulled the blanket over his shoulders. "Hey, let's see if we can name all of your favourite animals around town. Hmmm ... let me think ... there are the goats, and ..."

"Sheep and hens ..." Reuben started slowly, and then gathered momentum as he brought to mind all the animals he loved. The donkey at the end of the road. The chickens owned by the neighbours. He began to settle, and before he got to dogs and cats, his thumb was plugged firmly into his mouth, and he was fast asleep once more.

Miram lay beside her son for a long time that evening. Long after the servants themselves had gone to bed. She thought of John, her beloved husband. Oh, how she missed his embrace. Fresh tears slid silently down her cheeks as she stroked Reuben's hair.

"Who was here last night Miriam?" Uri wanted to know. "The maid said a messenger came to see you. Who was it, and what did they want?"

Miriam looked up in surprise. A feeling of dread washed over her from head to foot. Uri pinned her under his cold stare, and she knew there was no point in lying to him.

"Just a friend."

"A friend? What's his name?"

"Michael."

Uri raised his eyebrows. "The shepherd?"

"Well, he's a farmhand now I believe, but yes, the shepherd."

"Oh. How do you know him?"

"I've known him since I was a little girl. He's a friend."

"I see." Uri paused thoughtfully before continuing. "Well Miriam, as you are a dutiful wife, a good hostess and housekeeper, I do not want to be too hard on you. I know that it can be lonely here at times with only the servants for company while I'm away. But I cannot abide deceit. I will not have strangers coming around here at all hours. Friend or not, avoid a scandal."

"I understand. I'm sorry Uri. I did not invite him. He came of his own accord, and I sent him away promptly. I've told him not to return." She tried to keep her voice steady, but it cracked a little on the last word. Uri sighed.

"He may not under any circumstances come to this house. Remember, people are watching you. The town gossips never sleep, and if there is scandal, none of us will escape it." It took a long moment before Miriam was able to speak.

"I understand."

"Yes. I believe you do." She put her arms around the old man.

"Thank you," she whispered into his ear.

Chapter XXII

Cradle

Isaiah 54:4

*Fear not, for you will not be ashamed; be not confounded,
for you will not be disgraced; for you will forget the shame
of your youth, and the reproach of your widowhood you will
remember no more.*

You cradle billions of stars.
Scoop them up into Your hand.
Sprinkle like glitter dropped onto a canvas
Across the universe's expanse.

Incomprehensible greatness,
And yet ...
You care for each little seed.
Each flower in spring.
Each tiny sparrow
Is known by You intimately.

And unlike humanity's self-importance
That seems to reduce our ability to care,
The more that we comprehend Your Sovereignty,
The more that we can trust You are there.

For it's love that has birthed the stars
And given creation its boundary and form,
And it's the very same love that explodes,
At every new life that is born.

Kindness and mercy are woven deep
Into each unique frame and design,

And all ...
From the smallest to the greatest,
Will see Your purpose unfold in Your time.

Miriam – age 42

Miriam was happy to move back into her father's house after Uri passed away. His grown-up sons had arrived shortly before his death to say goodbye to their father, and more accurately, to lay claims to his wealth. The fact that Miriam had never met any of the five sons was very telling and Uri had warned her about them. While they were very much aware that their father had remarried several years earlier, her presence would be an afront to them. She was not their mother. Miriam decided it would be easier for her to step aside quietly. She had no interest in fighting them for any of Uri's property or possessions as such things had never truly interested her.

Reuban and Naomi helped her with the transition back to her father's house and asked few questions. They seemed to understand that it was necessary, and they all also relished the freedom of their small house on the edge of town. Such simplicity could not be found in the complications that came with much wealth.

Miriam, being older now, assumed she was free from the pressure of being married off once again. Her children had their friends and were part of the Sychar community. She knew that the consensus would be to view her as a poor widow and little more. A woman who had tried and failed in marriage, although the number of times she had been married was not something that even her closest friends were aware of.

Why give people more reason to gossip?

For the first time since she was a girl, Miram began walking the trails once again, up into the foothills behind the town. Only out there did she ever feel the weight of her own regret, shame, and grief truly lesson. Only out under open skies could she breathe.

One afternoon Miriam sat on the flat rock that overlooked the town. She had been there a while before she felt someone watching her, and turning sharply around, she was confronted by Michael.

"Mind if I sit down?" He sat before she could reply. "I'm surprised to find you up here Miriam."

"Well, I didn't expect to see you either," she replied. "I thought you were working somewhere else these days." She had not set eyes on him since the night she forced him to leave Uri's house.

"A man can't work all the time."

There was an awkward silence that followed. So much unspoken history sat between them. Miriam looked down towards the quiet town and then out at the horizon. She was not sure what to say.

"Miriam," Michael spoke quietly. "I want to apologise to you. I'm sorry that I made your life difficult when you first came back to Sychar. It was wrong and, well, it was selfish of me."

Miriam nodded. "Well, it doesn't matter now," she

smiled to let him know he was forgiven. "I'm the poor old widow that people will simply offload their charity to if they feel so religiously inclined."

"You're not old Miriam."

She laughed like it was a joke.

"I remember you as a young girl. So alive and full of joy. You used to run around up here like it was your own private garden."

"Wasn't it?"

Now Michael chuckled. "Well actually, perhaps it was. You certainly kept my sheep and I entertained on occasion."

Miriam smiled at the memory of herself as a young girl. Her mother had never really put a halt on her need to be out in nature. It had felt as normal to her as breathing and as important as her own soul.

"Can I ask why you left me Miriam?" He hesitated, then continued. "We could have found a way to marry. I know you know that. I also know that you did love me once. Yet instead of finding a way forward together, I suddenly discovered that you were already married to that bully of a man. If I never have the chance to ask you again, I'll kick myself for not having asked you now. I've wondered about it many times and it broke my heart all those years ago. A simple explanation will do. Please."

Miriam looked him in the eye and saw his tender heart and the unanswered questions that had lived in his mind for so long.

"You really don't know?"

"How could I know? You simply disappeared."

Something in Miriam snapped in that moment. There were truths in life worth speaking, simply because they were true. Only fear would keep her in the prison of silence, but Michael at least, had a right to know.

"I've told no one. No one at all, yet unfortunately that husband discovered it. I don't even like saying his name."

"Discovered what?"

"That I was pregnant."

"What?" The look of disbelief on his face shattered Miriam's heart.

"I was pregnant," she whispered again. "With your child." There was silence for a moment as the weight of the words sunk in. She continued. "I knew very well the reality and the stupidity of the situation we were in. I would have been stoned to death. The arranged marriage was a way I hoped to cover the whole situation from ever being exposed. I was trying to save both of us from what felt like an impossible situation. I'm sorry that I couldn't tell you Michael, but it was impossible. I was so terrified."

"I ... I can hardly believe it. Oh Miriam. You should have told me. We could have left here and gone somewhere far away to marry."

"I knew you'd say that. I was so scared Michael. I couldn't face running away. That just felt like more pain. More fear and uncertainty and I was terrified."

"But … you did run away. From me at least."

"I did. I ran into religion. Duty. Expectations. I thought I'd be safe behind those walls. I was wrong."

"Miriam…" Michael hung his head. "What happened to our baby?"

She sighed. "The baby died while I was still pregnant. Early on but too late for me because I was already married. Somehow that husband discovered the truth about the baby, that it was conceived before we married. He threatened me and my father. He divorced me quietly, but I had to leave Sychar."

Miriam could see the next wave of shock hit Michael. He moved close and put his arms around her. "I am so sorry."

A small piece of the numbness she lived beneath fell away under Michael's compassion. He would never know the whole of her story, but she was glad that she had been able to finally speak the truth about why she had left him all those years ago.

"Wait, I'm coming," Miriam called to Mary, Sheerah and Neriah as they walked past her home on the way to the well one morning. To Miriam's surprise, her friends kept going without turning their heads.

Perhaps they had not heard her?

They passed by her house on the way to the well every morning. Miriam usually waited outside for them, and they all walked together, talking about their lives and their children. But today she was running late.

Michael had come to visit her late the night before, and they had fallen asleep in each other's arms. He must have left before dawn and before the children woke, but she had overslept, and now her friends had gone on without her.

Miriam woke the children, got their sandals on, and chivvied them out the door, gathering her empty water jugs as she did so. She tried to hurry after the group, but the children put up a fuss and dragged their feet.

"I don't want to go. I'm too tired." Reuben complained.

"Me too," his sister added.

"Come on now, you both know we must go. I need your help to carry the jars."

"Can't we go later?"

"No. It's going to be a hot day, and I don't want to go out in the heat. We're already late. Please, hurry up."

The rest of the women were far ahead of them now, and with the two children slowing her down, Miriam knew she would never catch up. She sighed, shifted the water jugs into position on her hip, and walked on through the sleeping town along the well-worn path.

Every now and then she glanced over her shoulder to make sure that the children were following. They were deliberately dawdling in protest. She felt frustrated and irritable.

"I'm sure I never complained like this when I was a child," she muttered loudly enough for them to hear.

The heat meant that most people had collected their water early that morning and had headed home long before Miriam and the children got there. She did not mind the quiet though. She needed time to think. To process what had happened last night.

As she approached the small cluster of women standing around the well, they turned to stare at her. She walked over to Sheerah, Neriah and Mary, greeting them with a smile that died on her lips when her friends turned away from her. Miriam swallowed hard and carried on, trying to ignore the slight. There must be some explanation for their strange behaviour and she prayed it wasn't what she feared. Did they know?

"I called to you this morning. Didn't you hear me?" Mary glanced her way, shrugged her shoulders and turned her back on Miriam.

"I'm sorry I was late. I didn't know it would upset you so much," said Miriam trying not to show how much their behaviour unnerved her. Still, they made no effort to respond or even acknowledge her. "What is it? What have I done to offend you?" She came closer. They backed off, but not before Miriam caught a glimpse of Neriah's face.

Seeing the horror and disgust written large across her friend's features, Miriam suddenly knew exactly what was going on. There was no more room for denial. They knew that she had been letting Michael visit her late at night. Someone must have seen him enter her house. Perhaps last night they also saw that he did not leave. Someone had spread the word and now they all knew. The day of reckoning had arrived.

"Mary? Neriah? Sheerah?"

Neriah and Sheerah did not speak. They only gave Miriam a dark look and moved around to the other side of the well. For a moment a very heavy silence hung in the air.

"You're no longer welcome here," said an older woman whom Miriam knew only from a distance. Her name was Maya, and she was one of the town's foremost gossips. Miriam's mother had warned her about Maya's serpent tongue.

"What do you mean?" Miriam feigned confusion. Her heart was beating rapidly as she faced her worst fears, but she tried to maintain composure.

"We know you are a widow and that is sad. But now it seems you've decided to just live as a sinful harlot. That is not just sad, it is intolerable." The woman spat at Miriam and a ball of saliva landed on her left foot. "You're a disgrace to our town. You are lucky your father is not around to see this, but be warned, we will bring the matter up with the elders today." Miriam was shocked but also knew she shouldn't be. She looked expectantly at Mary, pleading for her to stand up for her as she always did.

"You should probably leave," Mary said with great sadness in her voice. "You must come to the well in the middle of the day when no one else is here."

Miriam's heart plummeted. She gathered her children behind her in a bid to protect them from the shame and condemnation that was being heaped upon her.

"If you're talking about the farmhand – he's just a friend. I've known him since childhood," she protested.

Some of the women scoffed, and Mary turned away.

"Don't embarrass yourself any further by denying the truth," said Neriah. "You have been seen with this 'friend' of yours. Last night, you allowed him to spend the night in your home – and you, a widow with two children in the house. Shame on you. Go now. Remove yourself from our presence."

Filled with righteous anger and bravado, the other women pressed in, telling her to leave and spitting at Miriam. Leaving her water jugs in the dust, she gathered her children's hands and pulled them behind her as she fled back towards the town.

When the fog of anger and shame finally cleared from her mind, true fear set in. She must find Michael and make sure that they got out of town before sunset, or they might all be brutally punished. Miriam would certainly be stoned to death as a harlot, and she could not even contemplate the fate of the children should she perish.

By that afternoon, Miriam and Michael had decided what they must do. They gathered her possessions amidst loud protests from the children and by sunset had moved into the small building Michael lived in on the farm he tended. It was outside the walls of the town. As long as she stayed out of sight, the critics would probably leave her alone.

"If they come, I will fight to defend you Miriam. And we will leave this place and start again elsewhere if we have to."

She believed him. Despite it all, facing the very thing she had tried to avoid her entire life, Miriam did believe that her friendship with Michael was now something she was willing to fight for herself. They would eventually marry, but until then, they had no other choice but to defy the religious laws and live shunned from the community. Their truth has been discovered too soon.

Isolated and trapped, the four of them embarked on an existence on the outskirts of town. Mercifully, Michael had been allowed to continue working on the farm, but only because the landowner was a lifelong friend. Even so, he gave Michael the dirtiest and most menial jobs. Michael never complained.

Miriam tried to make the shack as homely as possible while keeping the children occupied so that they didn't complain too much about not having any playmates. She bore her suffering herself without a word, knowing that this was the price she must pay for her sin. Her weakness. Her inability to conform to cultural demands. Shame followed her like a snake that was always ready to strike.

She avoided people whenever she could, but still felt their burning stares boring into her back. Try as she might, she could not close her ears to the razor-sharp insults flung in her direction – especially when they were directed at her children. These enraged her, but she dared not react or lash out, despite the injustice. One misstep, and the elders would exact their retribution.

Miriam felt as hollow and empty as the water jar she had left in the dust at the well. She was thirsty for the company of the friends she used to have, for acceptance into her beloved community, and for forgiveness for all she had done wrong in her life. She wondered whether she would ever feel whole and fulfilled again.

Every day, she made her shameful way to the well – alone in the heat of the day. Even though the sun scorched her head, and the sand spilled into her sandals and burned her feet, she always waited until midday to be sure no other women would be there.

Chapter XXIII

Living Water

Isaiah 12:1-6
In that day you will say:
"I will praise you, Lord.
Although you were angry with me,
your anger has turned away
and you have comforted me.
Surely God is my salvation;
I will trust and not be afraid.
The Lord, the Lord himself, is my strength and my defence;
he has become my salvation."
With joy you will draw water
from the wells of salvation.
In that day you will say:
"Give praise to the Lord, proclaim his name;
make known among the nations what he has done,
and proclaim that his name is exalted.
Sing to the Lord, for he has done glorious things;
let this be known to all the world.
Shout aloud and sing for joy, people of Zion,
for great is the Holy One of Israel among you."

You pour out in abundance,
Living waters over me.
Rivers of sweet mercy
That make it possible to breathe.

You refresh from a pure fountain,
Buried deep beneath the ground.
Living waters pushing forth
To nourish all that can be found.

Your Holy Waters wake me
From the slumber of my apathy.
With an unexpected pouring out
That stirs the sleeper who now sees.

For there is no one righteous.
Not a single living man,
Who can rise to meet Your Holiness
And in their own perfection stand.

Those who try to work for it
Work themselves into the dust,
While the flood of Your sweet Grace
Covers those who come with childlike trust.

The gravity of this heavy gift
Burns like fire within my hands.
Its weight much more than I can hold,
And yet by Grace it lands.

For you leave the ninety-nine
To find the straggler like me,
Who has stumbled time and time again
In rebellion and in apathy.

You pick me up so gently,
And walk me all the way back home.
Your shoulders now my resting place
That whisper I am not alone.

Your Mercy holds such power,
That impossible becomes the way,
As living waters freely flow
Upon the one You carry from the fray.

Miriam – age 43

The burning sting of sweat running into her eyes, snapped Miriam out of her reverie and she focused on finishing her work. She wanted to fill her jar and get away from the well as quickly as possible, not just because of the midday sun, but also because the place reminded her too much of better days. Days she knew she would never have again.

She was so intent on pulling the pitcher to the surface that she didn't see a group of men walking over the sands towards her. Sandaled, dusty, rough-looking men. If she had seen them, she would have sensed the danger and hurried away without bothering to finish filling the earthen jar.

Instead, she sat, exposed and vulnerable, as their silent steps brought them closer and closer.

Miriam jumped in fright when she heard voices behind her. She dropped the pitcher that fell all the way back down into the well, hitting the surface with a splash. Whirling around, she was horrified to find a large contingent of Jewish men, arguing about whether to go into town for food. She respectfully lowered her gaze and turned back towards the well. They all seemed to be ignoring her and Miriam kept her head down until their voices retreated. When she thought they had all moved away, she looked up, only to find that one of the Jews sat on the stone wall of the well. His frank appraisal made Miriam's cheeks burn. She snapped her head back down again.

Jews never acknowledged Samaritans and certainly never a Samaritan woman. She wondered why he was staring at her so openly. Was her presence here at this time of day telling the full story of her shame? The others had left, but she could not fathom why this one man stayed.

What was wrong with this one? She wished he would move so she could finish filling her jar and head home. Then it dawned on her. Perhaps he needed a drink and was waiting for her to move away so he could get one.

As though he had read her mind, he said, "Will you please give me a drink?"

Miriam gaped at him.

When she found the courage to speak, she blurted, "You are a Jew, Sir, and I am a Samaritan woman. How can you possibly ask me for a drink?" As soon as she'd said this, she realised how rude it sounded and wished she could take it back. But the stranger just smiled kindly at her.

"If you knew the gift of God, and who it is that is asking you for a drink, you would have asked me, and I would have given you living water," he said.

Miriam frowned. The man had obviously spent too long in the sun. He was not making any sense. Was he making fun of her? She almost felt sorry for him. Then she noticed he was empty handed. "Sir, you have nothing to draw water with and the well is deep. Where can you possibly get this living water?" She knew she was baiting him and should be ashamed of herself for talking back, but her frustration at being trapped in conversation with a stranger, clouded her judgment.

When he did not answer, she continued, unable to stop herself from trying to impress him with her knowledge of the well's history. "Are you greater than our father Jacob who gave us this well and drank from it himself along with his sons and his livestock?"

Why was she holding a conversation with this man? She wanted to leave but felt powerless to do so.

He seemed entirely unperturbed and in no hurry to move on. "Everyone who drinks from this water will be thirsty again, but whoever drinks the water I give them will never thirst again. Indeed, the water I give will become like a spring of water that wells up to eternal life."

Miriam laughed out loud. "Eternal life, you say?" She was now sure that this Jew must be crazy. "Oh, please give me this water so that I won't ever get thirsty again. I would give anything not to have to draw water every day."

"Go then," he replied. "Call your husband and come back."

Miriam's anger rose. The nerve of this man to talk to her this way. Who did he think he was going around promising eternal water to a clearly unhappy woman? Was he toying with her? Why? She balled her fists and spat out the words, "I have no husband."

With that she picked up the half-filled earthen jar and prepared to hoist it onto her hip. She had heard enough, but before she could position the vessel, he spoke again, his words stopping her in her tracks, "The truth is, Miriam, you have had five husbands, and the man you live with now is not your husband."

Miriam's eyes widened, and her jaw dropped. She was suddenly terrified. Was this some kind of trap before her trial and stoning? How did he know so much about her? How did he know anything about her at all? She peered at him, searching for some recognition. Had they met before? Her heart stopped cold. Had Alexander sent him? Or, perhaps he had been sent by the elders in the community who wanted to heap more judgment on her.

She had to get away from him quickly. She couldn't possibly take the weight of any more shame. And yet, he was confusing. She did not sense judgment and instead, his eyes were full of kindness. But, if he knew these things about her, how could he possibly show her compassion? Miriam's heart beat uncontrollably with fear, but she tried not to let him see it.

Sticking out her chin, she attempted to put on an air of polite disinterest, diverting his attention away from her and onto matters of religion once more. "Sir, I see that you are a prophet. Our ancestors worshiped on Mount Gerizim, but you Jews claim that the place where we must worship is in Jerusalem."

"Miriam," he replied, "believe me, a time is coming when you will worship the Father neither on the mountain nor in Jerusalem. You Samaritans worship what you do not know; we worship what we do know, for salvation is from the Jews."

Was he trying to condemn her for being a Samaritan? Was that what this was about?

Miriam had finally run out of words. She stood there silently, still wondering how he knew her name or that she'd had five husbands. He continued. "A time is coming, and has now come, when the true worshippers will worship the Father in the Spirit and in truth, for they are the kind of worshippers the Father seeks. God is spirit, and His worshipers must worship in Spirit and in truth."

"I know that the Messiah is coming," she boasted. "I've heard of Him. And when He comes, He will explain everything to us."

Then the man said something that stunned Miriam even more than the fact that he knew her name or the number of husbands she'd had. He simply said, "Miriam, I am He."

"What? What do you mean?"

"I am the Messiah."

She wanted to laugh again, but the look on his face stopped her. She felt the urge to run, but his presence restrained her feet. How could this simple, humble-looking man, possibly be the king they were waiting for? The very idea was absurd. She looked him up and down. His feet were dusty, his hair matted, and his clothes no better than most of the wandering homeless travellers who lived on hand-outs and charity.

"Miriam," he continued, "I assure you; I am He. I will prove it to you."

"How?"

"I know everything about you."

"That's not possible." Miriam's heart began to race, and she felt suddenly sick in her stomach. This must be a trap.

"I do," he smiled.

"No one knows everything about me. No one except God Himself."

"Exactly. I know that you loved your mother very much and were beside her when she passed away. I know that as a little girl you used to wander in the hills around Sychar, singing and playing. You loved the sense of freedom that the wilderness gave you."

Miriam's eyes widened and she sat down heavily on the stone wall, staring at this strange man. The water, her vessel, her troubles, everything faded into oblivion while he spoke.

"I know that when you were little, your father was hard on you and your mother, and for many years you were afraid of him. You longed for a sister or a brother, but you never had one. You had some close friends, and you met Michael when you were very young. He's the man you live with now. You care for him very much, but he is not your husband."

Uncontrollable tears began to well up in Miriam's eyes at the gentle reminders of her early years, and the unbelievable knowledge that this man seemed to have – not just about the events of her life, but about how she had felt. The contents of her heart were being exposed right in front of her.

"You never wanted to marry when you were young, and one of your deepest regrets is that you argued with your mother about it. You were afraid of living the life she had lived with your father. You regretted that the last few months you had with her were spent arguing over the issue – especially when your first husband Caleb turned out to be a good man."

"He loved you well, and you pinned your hopes on a future with him. You even let go of your feelings for Michael once you settled into life as Caleb's wife. You wished that your mother had known how happy you were."

"But you lost your first husband in a tragic accident, and you never have been able to make sense of it. You've asked how God could ever allow that to happen. You've been angry and disappointed with God, and you tried to run away from Him. You weren't just running from your life, Miriam. You were running from your disappointment with God, your Father. You couldn't make sense of how a loving God would have let such terrible events occur. You ran to Michael and for a little while you found comfort with him."

Miriam put her hands over her burning face. She felt lightheaded. *How could he possibly know about her time with Michael. Did he know about the child? Was this man real or was she hallucinating?* Perhaps the heat had finally made her crazy.

"It's okay, you don't have to be afraid. I do not condemn you like your husband Nirgal did. He abused you when he found out about the child. Then when you lost

Michael's baby, Nirgal divorced you because you could not give him an heir."

"I prayed so hard, for so long, and made sacrifices. Why did God not grant me another child?" She had always wondered, and this man seemed to know about everything, so she dared ask.

"If you'd had a child with Nirgal, you would have been stuck with him for the rest of your life ..."

"Yes."

"You must be thankful to God in all things − even when the answer to your most ardent prayers is 'no'. You must have faith that He knows best."

"You're very wise. How do you know so much about me? You are indeed a prophet."

"I know everything, Miriam. Nothing is hidden from me. I've always known you."

"Do you know how my life continued then? After Nirgal?" He nodded.

"You left and went to live with your aunt in Shechem, but you were still angry with God for taking Caleb and your mother from you. You had only started to heal when you met Alexander. Your aunt knew you were lonely and vulnerable, and she tried to warn you to stay away from him. You wanted to obey, but the temptation was too great. You made the sacrifices you thought would help. Remember that little white dove? But Miriam, your Father in Heaven does not need sacrifices. He only wants your heart."

"It was all I knew to do."

"I know. That's why I'm here."

"So, you … you know about …"

"Alexander? Yes. I know he promised you your heart's desires. He said the right words and painted pictures for you about a future you could hope for. He set lofty dreams above your head, and you put your faith in him, instead of putting your faith and your future in God's hands. He promised to marry you, but the marriage was built on false pretence. You know that now. He wanted you for darker purposes, and you paid a bitter price."

"I did."

"But Miriam, you know, the Father will never test you beyond your ability to endure. You have come through the fire, and you are stronger for it."

Miriam scoffed. "I may be stronger, but I am no less of an outcast."

"Your Father in Heaven will not cast you out. He loves you."

"How is that possible? Isn't it because of His laws that my own people have turned me out? My friends won't even look at me anymore."

"I know. And I know the pain that you carry in your heart because of this. But you have two beautiful children by John, your fourth husband," the man went on telling her story. "John was a good man, and he loved you deeply."

"Yes, and I loved him," she said bitterly. The memory of John made tears well up in her eyes. She brushed them away, hoping he had not noticed how deeply he had moved her. But the man did not seem at all uncomfortable with her emotion.

"If you could accept that John loved you despite your past, why can you not accept that God loves you and forgives you?"

She sighed. "John didn't know it all. He might not have been able to love me if he had known." Miriam felt hot, tired and bewildered by all this man was sharing with her. His voice was gentle and kind as he continued speaking.

"Uri, your fifth husband, was also a good man, though he knew he was not the husband you needed. Your marriage may have been one of convenience, but it worked well and benefitted both of you – or so it seemed. Though his intentions were good, Uri knew he would not be with you for long."

He paused before continuing. "So now, we come to your present day. When you continued to see Michael after Uri's death, and your affair came to light, the people of Sychar cast you, Michael, and your children out. You are living with that consequence and the shame you hold like it's a burden on your back. You feel it every morning when you rise. You feel it when you sleep. It is here, even as we speak."

Miriam felt a fresh wave of pain as he brought the truth to light. A heavy feeling of sadness had settled on her shoulders while he talked. Now it threatened to crush her under its weight.

"I also know something else about you, Miriam.

Something far deeper and more personal."

Could she take anymore of this?

"None of the men you have ever known – not even Michael – ever truly satisfied you."

She drew back, aghast at what he had just said. But he continued, "Deep within you is a thirst that none of them could quench. A void none of them could fill. They were just men. They could never hope to fill the emptiness you feel inside. That space is reserved for God alone. It is a spiritual void that only God can fill."

"What do you mean?"

"The sadness that weighs you down every day and presses on your chest every night is a part of your spiritual desire for fulfilment. The hollow feeling that sits in the pit of your stomach and never goes away, no matter what you do. The despair that makes you wonder whether life is even worth living. These are all signs pointing to the need for God to take His place in your life. Your Father in Heaven wants to fill the void inside you with His love and joy. He is the answer to all your needs. He will quench your thirst with living water from a well that never runs dry."

"I've never spoken to anyone about that emptiness and the desire for fulfilment. I've never even known how to put it into words."

"I know. But because God the Father and I are One, I can see into your soul. You are not a mystery to me as you are to others. Countless people live lives of desperation, just as you have – constantly seeking fulfilment. They are always reaching for things of this world to fill the void they feel inside. And the thing is, it does work – for a little while. Caleb was your rock – for a little while. Alexander made you feel amazing – for a little while. John gave you a sense of safety – for a little while. Michael gives you his love and it helps ease your pain – for a little while. But ultimately, none of them can offer the fulfilment you crave. Searching for love is like filling your jar at Jacob's Well. You must return every day because the water runs out and your thirst returns."

"So, you said you had another kind of water? Something that would fill me up and quench this longing. Something that would make me never thirst again. Where is it? Where can I find it?"

"I am your living water Miriam. I am Jesus, the Messiah. All you have to do is ask me, and I will fill you to overflowing – until you are so full of love and joy that you won't be able to contain it."

"But I am unclean. I am an outcast. A despised woman. I don't deserve to be filled with love and joy, only guilt and shame."

"I told you before, the Father and I are One. Your Father in Heaven loves you just the way you are. His love is steady and constant. It does not change with the seasons or with life's circumstances. His love is always enough. It doesn't mean that your life will be easy, but it means that you will have everything you need to live it well. His love is not dependant on you being good enough. I am the way,

Miriam. I am the Messiah, who will build a bridge for you to walk over safely."

"I ..." Miriam hesitated. She looked into his eyes and saw the purest compassion she had ever seen. "I believe you," she said, surprised at the truth of her own conviction. "Please give me this living water. I want to be filled with God's love."

He smiled. "I knew you would."

Chapter XXIV

Endless Flow

John 4:28-30

Then leaving her water jar, the woman went back to the town and said to the people, "Come, see a man who told me everything I ever did. Could this be the Messiah?"

Oh, how your kindness flows
Like pure rivers through my soul.
Gushing wild and running free,
Breaking mercy over me.

So, let me always only boast,
In the power that I know.
For I have seen first-hand,
The setting free to overflow.

I have felt the courage,
That surges from the source,
Where strength pours out abundant,
Like the commitment of a river's course.

It pays no heed to obstacles,
On the frontline of the fray.
Nothing is insurmountable,
For your justice always finds a way.

I have witnessed strength,
Held within Your hands,
And when released into my life,
I have the fortitude to stand.

You are the deepest artisan.
The only living spring.
Yet this is not a gentle trickle,
But a raging torrent I stand in.

For your power carves out gullies
And cuts trails into long dead ground,
Bringing life back to the desert
Everywhere I look around.

The violence of Your righteous shaking,
Goes forth to make a way,
Springing hope from desolation,
And calling back those gone astray.

Oh, how your kindness flows
Like pure rivers through my soul.
Gushing wild and running free,
And breaking mercy over me.

So, I will boast in You alone,
Jesus Christ, my Lord and King.
I bow my knee to You alone,
And praise to You I bring.

Miriam – age 43

Miriam was so engaged in conversation with the man at the well, that she was disappointed when the rest of the group returned with food in their hands. They saw their friend and Messiah speaking to her, but none said a word. She was somewhat surprised that not one of them questioned what he was doing wasting his time speaking to a lowly Samaritan woman. Instead, they tried pressing him to eat something.

The Messiah smiled at her, put his hand on her shoulder, and nodded. In that moment something in her heart released, as if the iron fist it had been held in, suddenly lost all power. The weight she had carried fell from her shoulders and a feeling of lightness and joy overcame her. Miriam knew something remarkable had happened in the encounter. She was free. She would never be the same.

As she stood from the wall of the well, Miriam felt a glow radiating from her very soul. Could the others see it? The feelings of love and joy were so all consuming she knew she could never hide or contain them.

"I have to go. I'm going to tell everyone about this." Jesus smiled and nodded as though he already knew she would declare this.

"She's allowed to go and tell?" one of the men questioned. "Why can she tell, yet we are still held in silence?" he seemed genuinely concerned.

"Because she is the one I have chosen," Jesus simply

replied. "She will be the first to declare that I am who I say I am."

Miriam smiled broadly at the group of men, unable to compose herself. "You have no idea!" She cried. "No idea of the bondage this man has freed me from. I must share this good news with others." Leaving her water container, she ran and skipped with joy down the trail, laughing as she went.

"Everything," she said aloud in wonder. "He knew everything about me, and He still loved me."

When she reached the edge of town, she began knocking on people's doors and calling out to them.

"You must come and meet this man. He's beside the well. I think He may be the Messiah. Come and meet the one we have been waiting for. He told me everything about myself – everything I have ever done."

A little crowd quickly gathered around her, their faces hard and suspicious, but Miriam glowed with confidence and love. Suddenly their judgment felt powerless, like it was nothing more than morning dew burned away by the sun. She continued telling them all about the Messiah who had come to the well – in Sychar of all places.

"What on earth is she talking about?"

"The heat must be affecting her."

"Should we go and see?"

"No one will be there. She's crazy."

"Listen to me," Miriam insisted. With the courage

of a young lioness who knows there is nothing to fear, she told them, "I met a man out by the well. He was so compassionate. So unbelievably kind. And He told me everything about myself from the time I was a child until now. There is no possible way other than the Lord himself, that he could have known such things. Issues of the heart. Things never spoken aloud."

They stared at her in amazement, and she looked back at them wide eyed. Instead of shame, she felt immense compassion. These people were not her enemies. They were sad and struggling people caught in religion and duty, but thirsty for hope – just as she had been.

"You must come," she exhorted them. "He has living water to give anyone who asks Him. And if you drink from it, you will never be thirsty again. This is what he said to me. Hurry, you must meet Him before He moves on. Go to the well. He's there right now. I'm going to tell everyone. No one should miss this."

She ran off down the road, singing and shouting the good news, knocking on doors and telling all who would listen about the Messiah at Jacob's well. When she reached Neriah's door, she hesitated, but only for a moment. She knocked and waited.

"Miriam? What is it? You know you shouldn't be here."

"Neriah, it doesn't matter anymore. I've just met a man and …"

"Oh Miriam. Stop. That's exactly what got you into

all this trouble. Will you never learn?"

"No, Neriah. It's not like that. This man is different. He ..."

"That's what you always say."

"Neriah, just listen. The man I met by the well today told me everything about my life – even things that I've never told anyone before. And some things that I didn't know myself but were nonetheless true. He showed me things I hadn't realised before. It was like he had walked beside me my whole life – right from the beginning. Then He touched my shoulder and took away all my shame. Now, I feel so full of love and joy that I just have to tell everyone about Him. Don't take my word for it. Go and see for yourself. He is just amazing and He's still out there by Jacob's well. You have to go and meet Him."

"You're crazy, Miriam. I'm not rushing out to the well in the heat of the day just to meet some strange man. You need to leave now." Neriah began to close the door on her friend. Miriam moved out of the way. She was saddened by her friend's rejection, but she had to go. She still had so many others to tell her story to.

As she skipped down the street, knocking on every door, Miriam was aware that Neriah watched her. "I think He's the Messiah. Could it be true? What if He is? Hurry over to the well, you don't want to miss Him."

"Help her to listen Father," she prayed under her breath. "Let Neriah have the chance to meet you today too."

People heard Miriam's cries and came outside to see what all the fuss was about. Some spoke quietly together; others muttered and shook their heads; while a growing number started slowly walking down the path that led to the well. Neriah was bewildered by what she saw. Were people actually taking Miriam seriously?

Meanwhile, Miriam exhausted the houses in one street and moved on to the next. She didn't want to miss anyone. She would tell everyone in the village before going to the market and finally the farm to find Michael and her children. She only hoped that by the time they got back out to the well Jesus would still be there.

Michael sat close to Miriam as they listened to Jesus. They were convinced that he was indeed the Messiah – it could not be otherwise. Crowds of people had come to him out by the well because of Miriam's story, and they had invited him to come back to town. The twelve men who travelled with him also came. Though clearly in awe of Jesus, they were rouges and ruffians, and Miriam found some of them a bit off-putting.

She marvelled at how such a simple man could captivate people the way he did. He was not loud or religious like the educated priests and scribes, yet he was extremely knowledgeable and wise. He did not possess anything of value, yet he carried himself with dignity, as though he were a king. He did not have any weapons to protect himself against those who might oppose him, yet he appeared to be fearless when it came to men. He treated everyone he met with respect and kindness.

Jesus had been in Sychar for only a day when the town gathered to hear him speak. He spoke about the Kingdom of Heaven, answered every question they posed to him, and inexorably drew everyone to him. No one had ever seen a man of such wisdom and grace before. Once they met him, they knew that he was the Messiah, the One they had all been waiting for. Everyone seemed to feel his kindness. He touched people and healed their ailments, confounding even the most cynical among them.

At sunset on the first day, Miriam still shone. Her shame had gone; her sins had been expunged; her time in exile was over. Following Jesus' example, the town had taken the four of them back into the fold. Their days as outcasts were over. Never again would she be held captive by shame and fear. She and Michael were going to be married by the end of the week.

Miriam recalled a dream she had as a young girl. A dream about an artesian spring in which a never-ending source pushed water up to the surface until the well overflowed. Pure, clean, and cool the water issued forth in an unceasing flow, so the well would never dry up. She remembered how, in the dream, she had been telling people that this water was for all of them.

Now she understood the meaning. She looked over

at Jesus. He was that artesian spring and he was right there in front of her, pouring out a never-ending stream of living water as he spoke and ministered to the people of Sychar. The water was his unending and unconditional love.

Jesus the Messiah did not judge and condemn even the worst sinner among them. He spoke of grace and told people that he was the only way to salvation. He said, none of them, not even the priests, would ever be good enough to find their way to Heaven. Only by believing in him would they find freedom from the bondage of sin and religious self-righteousness. People who had been held captive, just like her, could be set free and enter into eternal life through him.

Her smile deepened as she watched her children play at the edge of the crowd. Reuben sang as he ran in circles around his little sister.

What more could any mother want than to be able to teach her children a better way than the one she knew as a child?

She would teach them not to follow the futile pursuits that this world offered, or the confines of religious duty, but instead to accept the beautiful simplicity of his grace poured out for them. Her searching was over. She had found her source of joy. Her endless well of living water.

John 4 (NIV)

Jesus Talks With a Samaritan Woman

[1] Now Jesus learned that the Pharisees had heard that he was gaining and baptizing more disciples than John— [2] although in fact it was not Jesus who baptized, but his disciples. [3] So he left Judea and went back once more to Galilee.

[4] Now he had to go through Samaria. [5] So he came to a town in Samaria called Sychar, near the plot of ground Jacob had given to his son Joseph. [6] Jacob's well was there, and Jesus, tired as he was from the journey, sat down by the well. It was about noon.

[7] When a Samaritan woman came to draw water, Jesus said to her, "Will you give me a drink?" [8] (His disciples had gone into the town to buy food.)

[9] The Samaritan woman said to him, "You are a Jew and I am a Samaritan woman. How can you ask me for a drink?" (For Jews do not associate with Samaritans.)

[10] Jesus answered her, "If you knew the gift of God and who it is that asks you for a drink, you would have asked him and he would have given you living water."

[11] "Sir," the woman said, "you have nothing to draw with and the well is deep. Where can you get this living water? [12] Are you greater than our father Jacob, who gave us the well and drank from it himself, as did also his sons and his livestock?"

[13] Jesus answered, "Everyone who drinks this water will be thirsty again, [14] but whoever drinks the water I give them will never thirst. Indeed, the water I give them will become in them a spring of water welling up to eternal life."

[15] The woman said to him, "Sir, give me this water so that I won't get thirsty and have to keep coming here to draw water."

[16] He told her, "Go, call your husband and come back."

[17] "I have no husband," she replied.

Jesus said to her, "You are right when you say you have no husband. [18] The fact is, you have had five husbands, and the man you now have is not your husband. What you have just said is quite true."

[19] "Sir," the woman said, "I can see that you are a prophet. [20] Our ancestors worshiped on this mountain, but you Jews claim that the place where we must worship is in Jerusalem."

[21] "Woman," Jesus replied, "believe me, a time is coming when you will worship the Father neither on this mountain nor in Jerusalem. [22] You Samaritans worship what you do not know; we worship what we do know, for salvation is from the Jews. [23] Yet a time is coming and has now come when the true worshipers will worship the Father in the Spirit and in truth, for they are the kind of worshipers the Father seeks. [24] God is spirit, and his worshipers must worship in the Spirit and in truth."

[25] The woman said, "I know that Messiah" (called Christ) "is coming. When he comes, he will explain everything to us."

[26] Then Jesus declared, "I, the one speaking to you—I am he."

The Disciples Rejoin Jesus

[27] Just then his disciples returned and were surprised to find him talking with a woman. But no one asked, "What do you want?" or "Why are you talking with her?"

[28] Then, leaving her water jar, the woman went back to the town and said to the people, [29] "Come, see a man who told me everything I ever did. Could this be the Messiah?" [30] They came out of the town and made their way toward him.

[31] Meanwhile his disciples urged him, "Rabbi, eat something."

[32] But he said to them, "I have food to eat that you know nothing about."

[33] Then his disciples said to each other, "Could someone have brought him food?"

[34] "My food," said Jesus, "is to do the will of him who sent me and to finish his work. [35] Don't you have a saying, 'It's still four months until harvest'? I tell you, open your eyes and look at the fields! They are ripe for harvest. [36] Even now the one who reaps draws a wage and harvests a crop for eternal life, so that the sower and the reaper may be glad together. [37] Thus the saying 'One sows and another reaps' is true. [38] I sent you to reap what you have not worked for. Others have done the hard work, and you have reaped the benefits of their labor."

Many Samaritans Believe

[39] Many of the Samaritans from that town believed in him because of the woman's testimony, "He told me everything I ever did." [40] So when the Samaritans came to him, they urged him to stay with them, and he stayed two days. [41] And because of his words many more became believers.

[42] They said to the woman, "We no longer believe just because of what you said; now we have heard for ourselves, and we know that this man really is the Saviour of the world."

Other titles by Noleen Sanderson:

Hunting Angels – The Story of Uganda's Stolen Generation

ISBN: 978-0-6453697-5-5

Hunting Angels takes you on a journey into the depravity of civil war and the courage of the human spirit to survive and overcome against all odds. It gives a voice to the children from Northern Uganda whose stories need to be heard.